Mallory and the Ghost Cat

Mallory and the Ghost Cat
Ann M. Martin

AN
APPLE
PAPERBACK

SCHOLASTIC INC.
New York Toronto London Auckland Sydney

The author gratefully acknowledges
Ellen Miles
for her help in
preparing this manuscript.

Cover art by Hodges Soileau

ISBN 0-590-44799-8

12 11 10 9 8 7 6 5 4 3 2 1   2 3 4 5 6/9

Printed in the U.S.A.   28

First Scholastic printing, February 1992

CHAPTER 1

"That's mozzarella," I said, rolling my "r" so as to sound totally Italian, "not *mootsaroolie!*"

Claire giggled. "Mootsaroolie, meetsa-beenie, mouse-aroni" she sang, dancing around the kitchen.

I couldn't help laughing. Mouse-aroni sounded like a fast food for cats. Claire can be so silly sometimes. I guess all five-year-olds have their silly moments, but my little sister really takes the cake. I admit that there are times when I find her silliness irritating, but that night I was in a great mood, so I just went along with it.

"Okay, Miss Mouse-aroni," I said. "Bring that cheese over here and let me start grating it." We were making English muffin pizzas for dinner as a surprise for my mom. She'd phoned to say she'd be coming home late that night, because of a PTA meeting that was running overtime. I knew she'd be thrilled to find dinner on the table when she got in.

I was also steaming some artichokes, my favorite vegetable. They are *so* much fun to eat. You pull off one leaf at a time, dip it in melted butter or salad dressing, and scrape off the edible part with your teeth. I know, it sounds weird, but once you've tried them, you'll love them, too. We don't have artichokes too often — they're kind of expensive — but once in a while Mom will buy them for a treat.

"Okay, Claire," I said, "it's time to get out the English muffins. Can you bring them over here?" Claire loves to "help" in the kitchen, and even though her way of helping sometimes makes everything twice as complicated, I like to let her cook with me whenever I can. She gets such a kick out of it.

By the time Claire found the English muffins and danced them over to me, I'd finished grating the cheese. The tomato sauce (from a jar — I didn't have time to make it from scratch) was simmering. It was time to start the assembly line. English muffin pizzas are easy to make. All you do is open up each muffin and arrange the halves on a cookie sheet. Then you put a little tomato sauce on each one. Then you put some grated mozzarella (or meetsabeenie, if you prefer) on each one. Then you shake a little oregano on the tops, and into the broiler they go! Easy. And yummy.

But making them for my family is a bit of a challenge. Why? Because there are ten — yes, *ten* — people in my family. Claire is not my only little sister. I have two others. And I also have four younger brothers. So when I make English muffin pizzas for the whole family, I have to make four cookie sheets worth. And sometimes even that's not enough. English muffin pizzas are one of the few foods that everybody in the family agrees upon. All the Pikes love them.

That's us, the Pikes. I just realized that I haven't introduced myself. Here I am giving out recipes, and you don't even know my name. I'm Mallory Pike, I'm eleven years old, and I'm in the sixth grade at Stoneybrook Middle School in Stoneybrook, Connecticut. There. Now you know it all. Well, not *all*. There's a lot more I could tell you about myself, but it'll have to wait. First I want to finish telling about our dinner that Friday night.

Just as I was putting the last tray of pizzas into the oven, my little brother Nicky burst into the kitchen. He was *filthy*. His T-shirt was so muddy I could barely make out Dick Tracy, and his jeans were not only muddy but torn as well. "*What* have you been doing?" I asked, sounding just like my mother. I've been taking care of my brothers and sisters for so long that sometimes I *feel* like a mother.

Nicky looked about as guilty as an eight-year-old boy can. "Nothing," he said, shrugging. "Just playing mudball."

"*Mud*ball?" I asked. "That's a new one on me. Who thought up that idea?"

"I did," said Jordan, coming up behind me. "Or at least, I had the *basic* idea. Adam and Byron figured out a lot of the details." He sounded proud of himself. He *looked* disgusting. He was even muddier than Nicky. By the way, Jordan, Adam, and Byron are all ten. They're triplets!

"What smells so good?" Jordan continued, pretending not to notice my frown.

"English muffin pizzas," I said.

"Yea!" he shouted.

"But they're only for *people*." I went on. "Not for pigs."

Jordan rolled his eyes. "All right, all right," he said. "I'll go clean up. Come on, Nicky." He grabbed Nicky's arm.

"Hold on!" I said. "You better get those clothes off *before* you go upstairs. Mom'll be mad if you guys track mud all over the house." My mom's not a fanatic about housecleaning — nobody with eight kids can afford to be — but I knew she'd be tired when she got

4

home. And she wouldn't appreciate her home looking like a dirt-bike track.

Jordan and Nicky headed for the laundry room, and I directed Adam and Byron that way, too, when they came in. A few minutes later I heard a singsongy voice yell out, "I see London, I see France, I see Nicky-and-Byron-and-Adam-and-Jordan's underpants!" This was followed by a major storm of giggles.

"Margo!" I called. "Leave your brothers alone." I walked into the living room just as the boys were trooping up the stairs, dressed, surely enough, only in their underclothes.

"Yeah," said Adam. "Leave us alone. And anyway, boys don't *wear* underpants. We wear *underwear*."

"Underwear, bunderwear," said Margo. "Whatever it is, you look silly."

"Margo," I said, with a warning tone in my voice. "That's enough. Come help me set the table, okay?" Margo's seven, and I guess all seven-year-olds are pretty fascinated by underwear-sightings. But she's easily distracted too, and, like Claire, she enjoys "helping."

Just as she and I turned to head for the kitchen, I saw Vanessa float down the stairs, passing her brothers on the way. She didn't seem to notice the way they were dressed. In fact, she didn't seem to notice that she'd passed them. Vanessa wants to be a poet, and sometimes she gets very caught up in her own little world. She's dreamy, absentminded, and often totally unaware of whatever might be going on in the *real* world. At first we thought it was a phase, but she's been this way for a long time now, ever since she was Margo's age. Since she's nine now, I guess it's not a phase. It's just the way she is.

"Vanessa!" I called, snapping my fingers. "Wake up!" She looked at me, blinking. "How about helping Margo set the table?" I asked.

"Plates and napkins, forks and knives," she said, in her "poetic" voice, "these are the settings for our lives."

Whoa. Sometimes Vanessa can really be out to lunch. She goes for entire days speaking in rhyme, and a lot of what she says makes about as much sense as that little couplet did. I shook my head and rolled my eyes at her, but she followed Margo and me into the kitchen and started to get out the napkins, so I decided not to say anything. The best way to deal with Vanessa is just to let her *be* Vanessa, I've decided.

While Vanessa and Margo set the table, Claire and I finished up in the kitchen. And by the time the boys had gotten cleaned up, both of my parents were home. It was time to eat.

"Oh, Mallory," said my mom, when she saw the pizzas, the artichokes, and also the salad I'd thrown together at the last moment. "You're a lifesaver. This looks terrific!"

"Is she a Wint-O-Green Life Saver or a Tropical Fruit?" asked Nicky, giggling.

"She's a Tropical Nut!" said Jordan.

"A Bobical *Hut*!!" said Claire, a little hysterically.

"Okay, okay," said Dad. "That's enough. Your sister was kind enough to make dinner for you, so how about if we thank her instead of making fun of her?"

All seven of my brothers and sisters turned to me. "*Thank* you, Mallory," they said in perfect unison, and totally without sincerity.

"Now let's *eat*!" added Byron, racing for his seat at the table. The others ran after him, jostling each other as they pushed past me.

Honestly. Sometimes my brothers and sisters all seem so — so *immature*. I mean, I know they're just kids, and I can't expect too much. But I'm kind of *tired* of being a kid. I'm ready to be more grown-up. And it's hard around this crew. Not to mention my parents, who don't seem to want me *ever* to grow up. Oh, they love to give me responsibilities, like taking care of the others and cooking dinner. But otherwise, forget it.

The problem is, I've got this curly red hair (everybody else in my family has brown hair), and glasses, and braces. Most of the time I look like some geeky kid. The braces aren't that bad — they're the plastic kind — but they just make me *feel* ugly sometimes. So do my glasses. If I could get a cool haircut, and contacts, and have my braces taken off . . . I can almost see how I could look halfway decent. My dad keeps saying I'm going to be a "knockout" someday. But for now, he and my mom say I have to wait. Just like I have to wait until I can wear certain kinds of clothes (like miniskirts and leggings) and makeup (a little blusher is all I'm asking) and until I can stay out later on baby-sitting jobs. (I could use the extra money.)

I admit there are some times when I still like being a kid. I like the way my mom takes care of me when I'm sick. I love being read to. And once in a while I even like to play make believe. My best friend Jessi Ramsey and I sometimes pretend we're horses. (This a deep, dark secret.)

I have some friends who are a little older — they're in eighth grade — and they tell me that *everybody* feels this way at eleven. Kind of caught between childhood and the next phase. Teenagerhood? What *would* you call it? Anyway, it's a confusing time for me. Mostly I can't wait to grow up, but there are times when I feel more like Peter Pan, like I *never* want to grow up.

That night I was *not* feeling Peter Pan-ish. I was feeling like I'd had quite enough of my loud obnoxious siblings. I couldn't wait until dinner was over and I could go upstairs to read the book I'd checked out of the library that day. I'd been looking forward to it the whole time I'd been cooking dinner. It's called *A Wrinkle in Time*, and the plot is kind of hard to explain. I love the main character already, and I think it's going to be a really, really good book.

But just as the English muffin pizzas ran out, my dad ruined my plans by announcing that he and Mom had decided to have a family meeting when dinner was over. He looked serious. I looked over at Mom. She looked serious, too. Oh, ugh. I *hate* it when they look that way. It makes me nervous. Sometimes family meetings turn out to be about really horrible things. Like the time my dad got fired from his job. I didn't have too much time to worry what *this* meeting would be about, though. The boys cleared the table in record time. They must have been as eager as I was to just get the bad news over with, whatever it was.

We gathered in the living room. A tense

feeling was in the air, and the room was very, very quiet. Then Dad cleared his throat.

"Do you all remember the stories I've told you about my uncle Joe?" he asked, looking around at us.

"Uncle Joe," said Nicky. "Is he the one who gave you the puppy?"

"That's right," said Dad. "He brought me Spanky for my eighth birthday."

"And he used to take you fishing, right?" asked Jordan.

"Right," said Dad. "Uncle Joe was the greatest. The first thing he'd do, every time he saw me, was — "

"Pull a nickel out of your ear!" yelled Margo. " I remember now."

"Well, he didn't *really* find the nickel in my ear," said Dad. "It was a magic trick. But for years I believed that nickels grew in my ears and only Uncle Joe knew how to get them out." Dad was quiet for a moment, smiling at his memories.

"*Anyway*," said Mom, giving him a look.

"Oh, right," said Dad. "Anyway, Uncle Joe is pretty old now. He's been living in nursing homes for a few years. And recently, he was transferred to Stoneybrook Manor."

"Are we going to go visit him?" asked Claire hopefully. "Maybe he'll find *quarters* in *my* ears!"

"Well, actually," said Dad. "It's even better than that. He's going to visit *us*. A few months ago I wrote to him, suggesting that maybe he'd like a little vacation from the nursing-home routine once he arrived in Stoneybrook. And he wrote back to say that sounded fine. So he's going to come and stay with us for a month or so."

"Oh, boy!" said Nicky. "Neat!"

"But where will he sleep?" asked Margo. "Maybe me and Claire should let him have our room. We could move in with Mal and Vanessa." She sounded excited at the prospect, but the idea made me groan. Sharing a room with *one* sister is bad enough. I wasn't crazy about the idea of having two more move in. I was excited about Uncle Joe coming, but I was hoping Mom could come up with better sleeping arrangements.

"I think we'll just set him up in the den," said Mom. I heaved a secret sigh of relief. "He'll be comfortable there, and that way none of you will have to be shuffled around."

"Yea!" said Adam. "This'll be great! He can teach us magic tricks, and tell us stories about when Dad was a kid — "

Dad held up his hand. "Hold on, there," he said. "We're going to have to take it slow with Uncle Joe. He may not be quite the same as I remember him. The people at the nursing

11

home told me he sometimes gets a little depressed, a little cranky. At his age, I guess he's entitled, but let's not overwhelm him right away, okay?"

Adam nodded. He looked a little less excited.

I had heard the conversation, but I wasn't paying the strictest attention to it. As soon as Dad had spilled the news, I'd started to worry about something. With Uncle Joe here, would my parents need me to baby-sit? I love to babysit and I do it a *lot*. In fact, I'm in a baby-sitters *club*, which I'll tell you more about later. But sitting for my family is my favorite. And what if Uncle Joe's visit turned out to be permanent? *Jessi's* Aunt Cecelia came to stay, and before she knew it, Jessi didn't get to sit nearly as much for her little brother and sister.

I decided that the best way to deal with my worries would be just to ask, so I did. "Dad?" I said. "When Uncle Joe is here, will you — will you guys still need me to baby-sit?"

He smiled at me, and so did Mom. "Of course, honey," he said. "We'll always need you."

What a relief. As soon as the family meeting was over, I headed for the phone. My book could wait. I needed to tell my best friend the latest Pike family news.

CHAPTER 2

"So *when's* he coming?" asked Jessi, as we walked up the stairs. It was Monday afternoon, and we were headed for a meeting of that club I told you about, the Baby-sitters Club.

"Dad said on Sunday," I answered. "We have a lot to do before then, to get ready for him. But I'm excited. Maybe you can meet him someday soon."

"Great," said Jessi. "I'd love to. Anybody who knows how to find nickels in people's ears sounds okay to me!"

By that time we'd taken our usual places and we were waiting for the meeting to start. Everybody else had already arrived. Who's "everybody else"? Well, the members of the club are: Kristy Thomas, Claudia Kishi, Stacey McGill, Mary Anne Spier, and Dawn Schafer. And me and Jessi, of course. Kristy, Claud, Stacey, Mary Anne, and Dawn are those friends I mentioned earlier, the ones who are in eighth grade. They're thirteen. Jessi's eleven, like me.

Dawn, Mary Anne, and Claudia were sprawled on the bed. Stacey was sitting backwards on the desk chair. Jessi and I were sitting cross-legged on the floor. And Kristy was sitting in her place of honor, the director's chair. She had tucked a pencil over her ear, and she was watching the clock. As soon as the numbers clicked to five-thirty, she sat up straight and said, "Order!"

Kristy's the president of the club. Why? Well, mainly because the club was her idea. She thought of it back when she was in seventh grade. She and her friends baby-sat a lot, and she figured they might as well get organized. If they met a few times a week in the same place, parents would know when and where to call for sitters. At first there were only four members in the club; now there are seven of us — *nine* if you count our associate members, who don't come to meetings. The club's worked perfectly, right from the start. Parents love the convenience of it, and we love the steady business that comes our way.

Kristy's what they call a "born leader," *I* think. She has a lot of good ideas, and she knows how to put them into practice. She runs the club like a business — like a very efficient, *successful* business, that is. She figured out when we should meet (Mondays, Wednesdays, and Fridays from five-thirty to six), how to advertise (with professional-looking fliers that we hand out whenever we need more business), and how to keep a record of our jobs (we have to write up every job we go on in the club notebook). Plus a whole lot more.

It's kind of surprising that Kristy's such an organized person. Her home life is what you might call chaotic. She has two older brothers, Charlie and Sam; plus a little brother named David Michael; plus a two-and-a-half-year-old sister named Emily Michelle (she's Vietnamese — Kristy's family adopted her not long ago); plus a stepbrother and stepsister (their names are Karen and Andrew, and they only stay with Kristy's family part of the time). Kristy's grandmother, Nannie, lives with them, too. And of course there's Kristy's mom and her stepfather, Watson.

Kristy was unlucky enough to have a father who ran out on her family, but she was lucky to get Watson for a stepfather. He's a millionaire. Honest. Now her huge family lives in his mansion across town. At first, when her mom married Watson, Kristy didn't want to leave her neighborhood (she lived near all her oldest friends). But now I have a feeling she kind of likes her new life. Not that she's stuck up.

Kristy's the most "regular" person I know. It's just that she's come to love her stepfamily, so that mansion has become a real home.

Our club's vice-president is Claudia Kishi. As you might suspect from her name, Claud is Japanese-American. Her family's a little less complicated than Kristy's. It consists of just Claudia, her genius (really!) sister Janine, and their parents.

Claud's the vice-president since we hold our meetings in her room. Why? Because she has not only her own phone, but her own private phone number. So we tie up *her* phone instead of one that belongs to some adult. We also mess up her bed, try on her jewelry, and eat her junk food, but Claud doesn't seem to mind.

Claudia has a lot of junk food around because she loves it, and she has a lot of jewelry because she knows how to make her own! Claud's a *great* artist, with an outrageous sense of style. She knows just how to complement her naturally stunning looks (long silky black hair, almond-shaped eyes, and a *perfect* complexion) with the very coolest clothes and accessories. If Claud put as much energy into her schoolwork as she puts into her art and her outfits, she'd be making straight A's. But school just isn't that important to Claudia. She has her own priorities, and art is first on the list.

Claudia's best friend is Stacey McGill, the club's treasurer. Stacey's a math whiz, which makes her perfect for the job of collecting dues and keeping track of club expenses. It's easy to see why she and Claud are best friends: Stacey's probably the only girl in Stoneybrook who could compete with Claud for the "Coolest Dresser" title. She grew up in New York City (her family moved here when she was in seventh grade) and she is just about as sophisticated as you might imagine. She gets her blonde hair permed, wears makeup and nail polish, and always looks very well put-together. She seems to have some kind of secret pipeline that keeps her informed about what's hip, what's happening, what's "in." But she's not one of those cool people who make *you* feel like a dweeb because you're still wearing last year's fashions. Stacey's really, really nice.

Stacey's tough, too. She's had some hard times lately, but she's come through them well. Her parents got divorced not long ago, and her dad lives in New York. Stacey spends most of her time here in Stoneybrook with her mom, but she visits her dad as often as she can. The other thing that's been hard for Stacey is that she has diabetes. That means her body doesn't deal too well with sugar because this gland called the pancreas isn't working right. She has to be *really* careful about what she eats. Not only that, she has to give herself shots every single day. The shots are insulin, which is what her pancreas is *supposed* to be producing. I can't imagine where I'd get the strength to deal with having a disease like diabetes. Stacey never whines or complains, though. She's pretty incredible.

The secretary of the BSC (that's what we call the club most of the time) is Mary Anne Spier. I think she has the hardest job of anyone in the club. She has complete charge of our record book, which is where she keeps track of all our jobs. She also keeps track of our schedules; she knows what day I'm going to be at the orthodonist, when Stacey is going to be in New York with her dad, and what time Claudia's art lesson will be over. It's awesome! When a parent calls to set up a job, Mary Anne can tell at a glance which of us is free. She also keeps the record book up-to-date with clients' addresses, kids' allergies, and all kinds of information we like to keep track of.

It can be kind of hard to get to know Mary Anne, because she's pretty shy. But once you *do* get to know her, she's a really great friend. She's sensitive, a good listener, and a lot of fun. Maybe Mary Anne is shy because she's not used to being around a lot of people; she grew up with her dad. Mary Anne's mom died when Mary Anne was a baby, so her dad brought her up on his own. He used to be very, very strict about clothes and makeup and other stuff, but he's loosened up lately. I wouldn't say Mary Anne is an outrageously *trendy* dresser, but she does have a few cool outfits.

Another thing Mary Anne has is a boyfriend! His name is Logan Bruno, and he's one of those associate members I mentioned before. (The other one is a girl named Shannon Kilbourne, from Kristy's new neighborhood.) Mary Anne's the only one of us who's ever really gone steady, and even though the romance has had its rocky points, I think she and Logan make a good couple.

Remember how I said that Mary Anne is a great friend? Well, maybe that's why she has not one, but *two* best friends. One of them is Kristy, and the other is Dawn Schafer, the alternate officer of the club. But Mary Anne and Dawn are more than just best friends — they're stepsisters!

Here's how *that* happened: Dawn grew up in California, but her mom had grown up here in Stoneybrook. So when Dawn's mom and dad got divorced, Mrs. Schafer decided to move back to her hometown. Thanks to Mary Anne and Dawn, she rediscovered an old boyfriend from high school, started to date him, and ended up marrying him. Who was that old boyfriend? Mary Anne's dad. It makes a great story, doesn't it? So romantic.

Dawn may live in Stoneybrook now, but we still think of her as a California girl. She has long, pale blonde hair and big blue eyes. (Nobody would ever mistake her and the brown-haired, brown-eyed Mary Anne for *real* sisters.) She dresses as though life were a beach party — sporty clothes in bright colors. And she *acts*, well, I guess "mellow" is the only word for the way Dawn acts. She's pretty self-assured, *very* individualistic (she's got not one, but *two* holes pierced in each ear!), and she's as cool in her way as Stacey and Claudia are in theirs.

Dawn has a younger brother named Jeff, but he doesn't live in Stoneybrook. He did for a while, but he missed his dad a lot and he ended up moving back to California to live with him. I know Dawn feels sad about the way her family has been split up, but the Spier-Schafer household is a pretty busy one, so I don't think she spends much time dwelling on the issue.

As for her job in the club — well, "alternate officer" means that she is ready to take on any of the other members' jobs. So if Mary Anne can't make a meeting, Dawn becomes secretary. Or if Stacey isn't there, Dawn collects dues. (It's not too often that *Kristy* misses a meeting. She just loves being president.)

I bet you're dying to know what *my* job is. Well, Jessi and I are called junior officers, and we don't actually *have* jobs to do. Junior officer just means that we do almost all of our sitting in the daytime. Our parents don't allow us to sit at night, unless we're sitting for our own brothers and sisters. You know what? I don't really mind being a junior officer, for now. I get plenty of work, and the other members are grateful to us for freeing them up for evening jobs.

Jessi doesn't mind, either. She doesn't like to stay out late anyway, since she needs to get enough sleep every night. She's a dancer — she studies ballet — and that's like being an athlete. You have to be in really good shape to be a ballerina, and *that* means not only getting enough sleep, but also eating right and taking care of your body in every way.

I'm not sure I'd ever have that kind of dedication, but Jessi does. She works really, really hard at her dancing (her classes are *serious*) and I think she might be a famous ballerina some day. (Maybe when that happens, I'll write a book about her. That's what *I* want to do when I'm older — write and illustrate children's books.) Jessi's family is very encouraging and supportive of her. The Ramseys are great. They're a really close family. Besides Jessi, there are her parents, her little sister Becca, and Squirt, who's her baby brother. And, as I told you before, Jessi's Aunt Cecelia recently came to live with them, too. At first we thought she was a total monster, but it turns out that she's not so bad.

We should have known better when we first judged Aunt Cecelia. We were being unfair. It was like when people made judgments about the Ramseys when they first moved to Stoneybrook. Just because the Ramseys are black, people were ready to think all kinds of terrible things about them. There aren't too many black families in Stoneybrook, and when Jessi's family arrived, people weren't all that nice to them. But I think the Ramseys are pretty well accepted by now. Isn't prejudice awful? If people only knew how much it can hurt.

Anyway, I'm getting off the subject here. I just wanted to explain a little bit about who's in our club and how the club works. So now you know! Our meeting that day was pretty routine, except for one phone call near the end. It was from a Mr. Craine. The Craines had not been clients of ours before, but Kristy knew who they were. Her mom plays tennis with Mrs. Craine.

Mr. Craine was calling to line up a regular sitter for his three daughters. He explained to Kristy (who had answered the phone) that the girls had a favorite aunt who usually took care of them, but that she'd just broken her leg. The Craines were going to need someone to sit for the girls on a regular basis until their aunt's leg was better. Mr. Craine said he was hoping the girls could have the same sitter all the time "since they need that kind of continuity," and that most of the jobs would be on afternoons and weekends.

Guess why I'm telling you all of this. Because I got the job. Or should I say jobs? I went home feeling pretty happy and excited that day, happy that I'd have plenty of work for a while, and excited because new clients are *always* exciting. I couldn't wait for Saturday, when I'd go to my first job at the Craines'.

CHAPTER 3

Drip. Drip. Drip. Oh, no! It had started to rain. I had been having such a good time, too. My friends and I were having a picnic in a beautiful meadow. I was eating fried chicken, and watching Jessi fly her kite. Then the rain started. *Drip. Drip. Drip.* I felt it rolling down my face.

I wrinkled my nose, then threw my arm over my face, trying to avoid the drops.

"Stop for a second!" I heard somebody hiss. "She's waking up."

My brain began to clear, and the picnic scene dissolved. I opened one eye. I wasn't in a meadow with my friends. The picnic had been a dream. I was in my bed, and I was surrounded by four grinning boys. One of them made a furtive move to hide what he was holding, but I was able to catch a glimpse of it.

"What's that you've got there, Jordan?" I asked. "Hmmmm. . . . An eyedropper filled with water. *Very* interesting."

Byron, Adam, and Nicky giggled. Jordan looked nervous.

"We — we just wanted to wake you up," he explained. "Uncle Joe's coming tomorrow, remember? We have a lot to do!"

"And you thought the water-torture method would be the best way to wake me up?" I asked.

Jordan nodded. "It *did* work pretty well," he said.

"Oh, it did, did it?" I asked, trying to sound menacing. I put on a big frown and threw off my covers. "Well, I'll teach *you* a lesson about waking up big sisters by dripping water all over them!" I said, reaching out and grabbing him. I pulled him onto the bed and started to tickle his belly.

"Stop!" Jordan shrieked. He giggled madly as I continued to tickle him.

"Not until you promise never to do it again!"

"Okay, okay!" he said, breathless. "I promise!"

"*I* don't!" yelled Byron, jumping onto the bed. Adam and Nicky weren't far behind. Soon my bed was a mass of squirming, giggling, shrieking boys. Everybody was tickling everybody else. We were having a blast. This may not be the way that most *normal* families start their Saturday mornings, but in the Pike household it's not out of the ordinary.

Vanessa didn't even blink an eye when she came to the door and saw us. "Come on, you guys," she said. "I've been up for *hours*, helping Dad make waffles. It's time for breakfast."

"Waffles!" yelled Byron.

"Yea!" shouted Adam.

"Yum!" said Nicky, licking his lips. "I want strawberry jam on mine."

"What am *I* going to have?" asked Jordan. Jordan doesn't like waffles, as strange as that may sound. He's the only person I ever met who doesn't. But, as I said before, there aren't many foods that all the Pikes agree upon. And my parents don't try to make us eat things we don't like. They figure they'd spend way too much time arguing with us if they tried to enforce rules about food. So they just stock up on a lot of healthy stuff, and everybody is allowed to eat whatever they want.

"How about if I make you a peanut-butter-banana-and-salami sandwich?" I asked. "Just to prove that I forgive you for waking me up that way."

"All right!" said Jordan. He *loves* that disgusting combination. In fact, he invented it, and he's very proud of the fact. He even sent the recipe for it ("Take two pieces of bread and toast lightly . . ." it begins) to a "Stupendous Sandwiches" contest in some magazine. He never did hear what the judges thought of it. I guess they were too busy taking Alka-Seltzer.

"Mmm, those waffles smell great, Dad," I said as I walked into the kitchen. I went right to work on Jordan's sandwich.

"Well, we have a busy morning, so I thought we should eat a hearty breakfast," he said. "Why don't you grab a plate and sit down? This batch is just about done."

As soon as Jordan's sandwich was ready, I gave it to him. Then I brought my plate of waffles into the dining room and sat down next to Margo. She was eating a bowl of Cheerios, with blueberries sprinkled on top.

"Didn't you feel like waffles today, Margo?" I asked. She can be a picky eater; a food she loves one day will seem totally unappetizing the next.

She shook her head. "Nope." She toyed with her cereal, using her spoon to chase the blueberries around the bowl. "Anyway, I like the way the blueberries turn the milk purple," she said. "Isn't it beautiful?" She sounded dreamy. "Ms. Cook says that purple is her favorite color," she added. Ms. Cook is Margo's teacher, and Margo is *crazy* about her. Sometimes I get tired of hearing about Ms. Cook.

"Just lovely," I answered.

By the time Dad finished making all the waffles and had a chance to sit down and eat some himself, the rest of us were almost done with breakfast. Adam ate the last bite of his waffle and stood up. "Hold on!" said Dad. "We have to make some plans." Adam sat down again and looked expectantly at Dad. "Uncle Joe will be coming at about ten tomorrow morning," Dad went on. "It would be nice if his room was ready by then. We'll need to — "

"Do you think he'll show us that trick where he turns a handkerchief into a mouse?" interrupted Claire.

"He might," said Dad. "If you ask nicely. I'd forgotten that I told you about that trick. Boy, he was good at that. He could really make it look like this little mouse was running up his arm . . ." Dad looked kind of happy and faraway, as if he were remembering something wonderful." And he was great with animals," he went on. "He helped me teach Spanky some of the most amazing tricks. Did I ever tell you about the one where — "

"Where Spanky would play dead until somebody said the magic word?" asked Adam. "I remember that story. I wish we had a dog, so Uncle Joe could teach it to do stuff like that."

"Maybe he could teach Frodo some tricks," said Claire.

We all laughed, and Claire looked hurt. "I'm sorry, Claire," I said. "It's just that hamsters aren't like dogs. They aren't so good at learning tricks. Mostly they just want to eat and sleep and run on their wheels."

"Sometimes Frodo stands on his hind legs," mused Jordan. "I wonder if he's trying to do a trick then."

"I think he's just trying to get out of his cage," said Adam. "He likes to run around in our room and hide under stuff."

"Okay," said Dad. "We're off the subject here. I'm sure Uncle Joe will be happy to meet Frodo, but for now what we need to figure out is how we can make the den into a comfortable bedroom. The couch in there pulls out into a perfectly fine bed, so that's all set. And I'm going to put up some hooks for Uncle Joe to hang his clothes on. Does anybody else have ideas about what we can do?"

"I think we should take your desk out of there and put in a night table instead," said

Mom. "That way he'll have more room, and you won't have to bother him if you need to work at your desk."

"Good idea," said Dad. "What can we use for a night table?"

"How about my toy chest?" asked Nicky. "I never use it anyway." *That* sure was true. The boys' room looked like a toy store that had been hit by a small tornado: G.I. Joes, Ninja Turtles, and Hot Wheels were strewn over every surface.

"I think my bookshelf would be better," said Jordan. "It has more room to store things."

"No!" said Nicky. "I want him to use my toy chest!"

Jordan drew a breath, but before he could say anything, Mom spoke up. "Let's try not to get into any arguments," she said. "It's exciting to have Uncle Joe come stay with us, but it's a big change, too. Things are going to be different around here, and we'll have to make adjustments. Let's try to work *together* on this, okay?"

"Okay," said Nicky. "But I still want Uncle Joe to use my toy chest," he added.

"I think that'll be fine," said Mom, with a warning glance at Jordan. "And maybe you three boys would like to contribute some artwork, to make the room cheery for Uncle Joe?"

"Okay," said the triplets.

"I'm going to draw Leonardo fighting Shredder," said Byron.

"I'm going to draw Calvin and Hobbes," said Adam.

"I'm going to draw a picture of Uncle Joe," said Jordan. He paused for a moment. "What does he look like, anyway?"

"Good question," said Dad. "I haven't seen him in years. I remember that when I was a boy, I thought Uncle Joe looked like he should have been a cowboy. He had this rugged face, and clear blue eyes that — "

"Ahem," said Mom. "How about if we get to work?"

"Right!" said Dad. "Okay, Nicky, let's go get your toy chest. Then we'll need some help — " he looked over at me " — moving that big old desk out of there."

"I'll dust everything," said Vanessa. That's the one cleaning job she likes to do. She takes the big feather duster and waltzes around dreamily, dusting here and there. Sometimes she forgets to finish one room before she starts the next, but she does her best.

"I want to make a special surprise for Uncle Joe," said Margo.

"That's nice," said Mom. "What kind of surprise?"

"It's a secret," said Margo. I could tell she was trying to sound mysterious.

"A secret?" asked Claire. She *loves* secrets. "Can I help?"

Margo started to shake her head, but Mom gave her a Look. "It would be a big help if you would let Claire work on the surprise with you," she said.

"Oh, okay," said Margo. "But you have to promise not to tell what it is until it's done," she said to Claire.

"I promise!" Claire and Margo headed off for their room.

The triplets were already busy in the rec room, where they keep their art supplies. Making "art" for Uncle Joe's room would keep them occupied for hours. Finally, everybody had a job. The house buzzed with activity for the rest of the morning.

I helped Mom neaten the den, open out the couch, and make the bed. I helped Dad move his big desk out of the den and into a corner of the dining room. I sent Vanessa, who had finished dusting, to get a set of clean towels to put out for Uncle Joe. Once in a while, I checked up on the triplets and on Margo and Claire. And all day I wondered about what it would feel like to have another person living with us — an older person. I haven't spent much time with old people, because my grandparents all live pretty far away, so I don't really know how to act around them. I'd seen those shows on TV where the kindly grandfather teaches the kids lessons about life, but somehow I wasn't convinced that those shows were always so realistic. I had a feeling that having Uncle Joe around might take some getting used to.

It wasn't long before the room looked clean and homey. The bed was made up with fresh sheets, and the covers were turned back invitingly. We'd set a small reading lamp on top of Nicky's toy chest, and Dad had hung a row of hooks along the wall. The triplets had made a big deal about putting up their artwork, and I had to admit that their pictures looked cheery and bright.

Margo and Claire were still hard at work on their project as I got ready to leave for my sitting job with our new clients, the Craines. I heard them giggling, and at one point a paint-splattered Claire wandered into my room and asked me to show her how to draw a tulip. I had no idea what they were up to, but I decided to let Margo keep her secret for the time being. Everything else was all set for Uncle Joe's arrival. I was sure he was going to feel welcome at the Pike household.

CHAPTER 4

"Thanks for your help, Mal," said Dad. "I think Uncle Joe will be really pleased to find such a comfortable room waiting for him."

"I hope so," I said. I watched the windshield wipers glide back and forth. The day had turned gloomy, so Dad was driving me over to the Craines'. By the time we'd turned out of the driveway, the rain had begun. And now the wipers could barely keep up. Suddenly it was *pouring*. "Boy, I'm glad I didn't ride my bike," I said. "I'd be drenched by the time I got there."

"Did I ever tell you about the time Uncle Joe and I got caught in the rain?" Dad asked.

I gave a little sigh. I'd been hearing an *awful* lot of Uncle Joe stories lately. But I didn't want to hurt Dad's feelings. "I don't think so," I said. "What happened?"

"We were walking to our favorite fishing hole," Dad said, "and it started to pour, just like it is now. We got soaked. Most grown-ups would have turned around and gone home, but not Uncle Joe. Instead, we kept heading for the fishing hole, and when we got there, we both jumped in, clothes, fishing poles, and all — just for the heck of it!"

I laughed. "Your mom must have been pretty mad when you came home all wet," I said.

"Nope!" Dad was grinning. "She never found out. The sun came out as soon as the storm was over, and we were bone dry by the time we returned home. We brought her a couple of beautiful trout for dinner, too." Dad was getting that faraway look in his eyes again. If I didn't stop him soon, I'd be in for five more stories about Uncle Joe. Luckily, we were almost at the Craines' by then, so I started reading off house numbers, looking for number ninety-four.

"There it is!" I said, pointing to a big white house.

"I've noticed this house before," said my dad. "I've always liked the way the porch wraps around the front and side of it." He stopped the car and turned off the engine.

"What are you doing?" I asked. "You don't need to park. I'm just going to jump out."

"I thought I'd walk you to the door, as long as I'm here," said Dad. "Since they're new clients and all. I'd like to meet them, just so I know who you're sitting for."

Oh, my lord. I couldn't believe it. How humiliating! Actually, I knew he was right, but I felt he was treating me like a baby. Would anybody else's dad do it? Then I remembered something that Kristy had said at a meeting not too long ago. "It's a good idea to have a parent or someone else with you when you meet a new client for the first time," she'd said. "Just to be on the safe side."

Oh, well. Whether Kristy and my dad were right or not, I had no choice. Dad had already climbed out of the car. He was getting ready to march up the walk, so I joined him on the sidewalk, and we headed toward the house.

I rang the bell and stood there waiting, with Dad beside me. I felt like I was going to die of embarrassment. The Craines would probably think I was just a kid *myself*. What if they decided that I was too young to watch *their* kids? But when Mr. Craine opened the door, I could see right away that everything was going to work out. He smiled at me and said, "Hi, Mallory! Glad to meet you. I'm Mr. Craine." Then he turned to my dad. "You must be Mr. Pike. I'm sure I've seen you at PTA meetings, but we've never introduced ourselves. Would you like to come in for a minute? I don't think Mrs. Craine is ready to leave yet."

Well, at least he didn't seem to think that it was weird for my dad to walk me to the door. But I sure didn't want Dad to settle in for a visit. I mean, what if he started in on one of his Uncle Joe stories or something? I shot Dad a look, and he gave me a little nod to show that he understood.

"No, I've got to be on my way. It's nice to meet you, though," he said to Mr. Craine. "Have fun, honey," he added, smiling at me. Then he left. Finally.

"Well, come on in, Mallory," said Mr. Craine. "The girls are dying to meet you." I followed him into the kitchen and saw three curly-headed girls sitting around a big table, coloring. They looked up at me shyly.

"Girls, this is Mallory," said Mr. Craine. "Mallory, I'd like you to meet Margaret, Sophie, and Katie."

"Hi!" I said. "What are you guys drawing pictures of?" I approached Margaret, the oldest, and peered over her shoulder. "Wow," I said. "That's a great picture of a horse. I love horses, but I can't draw them nearly that well."

Margaret beamed at me. "Know what? I'm six," she said, "and Sophie's four, and Katie's two and a half. How old are *you*?"

"I'm eleven," I answered.

"Wow," she said, "You're *old*. But you know what else?"

"What?" I asked.

"My mom's even older than you. She's thirty-four!"

Mr. Craine laughed. "I don't know if Mommy would like you telling everybody how old she is," he said.

"I only told Mallory," said Margaret. "Anyway, Mommy doesn't mind. She said so."

"That's right," said Mrs. Craine, walking into the room. "I'm proud of my age!" She stuck out her hand. "Hi, Mallory, nice to meet you. The girls are getting over colds, so I think they'll be pretty quiet today. But don't be fooled. These little princesses can run you ragged when they're feeling well."

"That's what Aunt Bud always says," explained Margaret.

"Aunt Bud?" I asked.

"Margaret will tell you all about her, I'm sure," said Mrs. Craine. "We have to get going. I left the number where we'll be, plus some other information, on that pad by the phone. The girls should take a nap soon, since we want to make sure those colds are gone. Have fun, girls!" After a round of hugs and kisses, the Craines were out the door and I was alone with my three new charges.

The second the door closed, Katie began to cry. "Want Mommy," she sobbed. "Want Mommy."

"Mommy will be back soon," Sophie told her, before I could even open my mouth to say the same thing. These girls were used to taking care of each other; I could see that right away.

"And maybe she'll bring us a present," said Margaret.

Katie stopped her sobbing for a second to think about that possibility, but then she started up again. I held out my arms to her and she climbed off her chair and into my lap. She must have needed a hug, and she didn't seem to mind getting one from a stranger. She was still sobbing gently as I held her and stroked her back.

"Tell me about your Aunt Bud," I said to the girls. I figured a little conversation might distract Katie.

"She's our *regular* baby-sitter," said Sophie.

"She's really, really fun," said Margaret. "She likes to be silly."

"Vroom, vroom," said Katie.

"What?" I asked.

"She said vroom vroom," explained Margaret. "That's because Aunt Bud usually rides over here on her motorcycle!"

"Wow," I said. "Neat. A motorcycle-riding aunt." I imagined a kind of tough-looking woman with a leather jacket and big black boots. "Is that how she broke her leg? Riding her motorcycle?"

"Nope," said Margaret. "Her dog broke her leg! He was so happy to see her one day that he ran right into her and knocked her over. But she wasn't mad at him. She says it wasn't his fault."

I had to ask one more question about Aunt Bud. "How did she get that funny name?"

"It's not her *real* name," said Sophie.

"Her *real* name is Ellen. But my daddy always calls her Bud," said Margaret. "She calls *him* Bud, too. They're Buds. That's a special kind of friend. We're all Buds, too!" She held out one pinky finger to Sophie and one to Katie. "This is the special Bud shake," she explained as they linked pinkies.

I smiled. "Cool," I said. By then, Katie had stopped crying. "How about if you Buds finish up your drawings, and then it'll be time for a nap?" I asked.

"Yucko," said Margaret. "I hate naps."

"Yucko," echoed Sophie.

"Uck," said Katie.

"Hmmm," I said. "I used to hate naps, too. But you know what's fun? Having a slumber party! Did you ever do that?"

Margaret shook her head. She looked perplexed, but interested. "How do you do that?" she asked.

"Do you guys have sleeping bags?" I asked. If they didn't we could just use blankets, but I knew that sleeping bags made the game even more fun.

Sophie nodded. "We got them for Christmas this year," she said. "Mine has Barbie on it."

"Mine has the Simpsons," added Margaret. "And Katie's has Muppet Babies."

"Great," I said. "Let's go get them and bring them into the living room." I followed the girls to their rooms and helped carry the sleeping bags downstairs. Then we arranged them on the living room floor. "Okay," I said. "We're almost ready to start our slumber party. We just need one more thing. Can you guess what it is?"

"Pillows!" yelled Sophie.

"That wasn't what I was thinking of," I said, "but pillows are a good idea. I'll go get them for you in a minute. The thing I was thinking of was a snack. When my friends and I have slumber parties, we always have snacks before we go to sleep."

"Yeah, snacks!" said Margaret.

"Cheez-its!" said Katie, leading the way back to the kitchen. She pointed to one of the cabinets. I filled a bowl with crackers and herded the girls to their sleeping bags.

"Okay," I said, "everybody get cozy, have some crackers, and then I'll read you a story." As the girls snuggled into their bags, I found their pillows and then checked the bookshelf for a story they'd all like. I found a copy of *Rapunzel*, which seemed perfect. And it was. Before I'd even finished the book, Margaret, Sophie, and Katie were fast asleep.

I had brought *my* book, *A Wrinkle in Time*, with me just in case I had time to read. It was in my jacket pocket, and my jacket was in the hall closet. I went to find it. I hadn't really expected to have a chance to read, and I was happy to be able to spend a few minutes with my book. The characters were beginning to seem so real to me. I couldn't wait to get back to it.

Just as I reached into my jacket pocket and grabbed the book, I heard a strange noise. At first I couldn't figure out what it was. A bird? Katie crying? I listened again, but all I could hear was the rain pounding on the roof. Then, as I turned to go back to the living room, I heard it again. Finally I realized that it was a cat, but its voice was very weak and small.

I thought it was kind of funny that the Craines hadn't mentioned that they owned a cat — usually new clients let us know about whatever pets they have. But it didn't really matter. I listened once more, but when I didn't hear anything, I took my book and headed for the living room couch.

It was very peaceful, sitting there with the three girls sleeping on the floor nearby. The rain beat against the windows, and the trees outside were tossing in the wind, but I felt warm and cozy on the couch. I opened my book and started to read.

Then I heard it again. That cat. It kept meowing, in a pathetic little voice. I put my book down, reluctantly, and listened carefully. The cat meowed again, and this time I had a feeling that something was wrong. Was the cat sick, or hurt? I wasn't sure what to do. "Here, kittykittykitty!" I called softly. "Come here, little kitty!" I heard another meow, but no cat appeared.

I got up and started to walk around the house, checking under chairs and couches, and opening closets in hopes of finding the cat. I whistled now and then, and called a few times. By the time I'd walked around the first floor, the meowing had finally stopped. I still hadn't found the cat, but I decided it was time to give up. I headed back to the couch and picked up my book, but before I could read even a sentence, Margaret sat up, rubbing her eyes.

"Hi," she said. "Can I get up now?"

"Sure," I replied. I helped her roll up her sleeping bag, and by the time we were done, Sophie and Katie were also awake. The three of them wanted to do some more drawing, so we went back to the kitchen table. I picked up a crayon and doodled a cat on a piece of construction paper.

"Hey, you guys," I said, "where does your cat usually hide, anyway? I looked all over for him this afternoon."

Margaret glanced at me with a blank look on her face. "We don't have a cat," she said. Then she went back to her drawing.

No cat, huh? I shrugged. I had no idea what else could have been making that meowing sound, but it didn't really matter. I was enjoying sitting for the Craine girls, and I had a lot more time with them to look forward to. I crumpled up my cat doodle and started drawing a picture of Uncle Joe and Dad (as a boy), walking down the road with fishing poles over their shoulders. I couldn't fill in Uncle Joe's face yet, but I knew that by the next day I'd be able to. I couldn't wait to meet him.

CHAPTER 5

Sunday did *not* dawn bright and sunny. It dawned gloomy and gray and drizzly. In books exciting days usually start off beautifully, but in real life, it's just as likely to rain. Still, I felt cheerful as I got up and got dressed. Mom and Dad were going to pick up Uncle Joe when breakfast was over, and I could hardly wait.

Everybody else was pretty excited, too. Breakfast was a wild scene. Dad hadn't had time to make waffles again, so it was every man (or woman, or boy, or girl) for himself (or herself, or — oh, forget it). There were about four boxes of different kinds of cereal on the table, plus a loaf of bread, a jar of peanut butter, and a big bowl of fruit.

Breakfast isn't usually an especially quiet time in the Pike house, but that morning it was especially noisy. Even when I lifted my cereal bowl right to my ear, I couldn't hear that snap, crackle, and pop. The sounds were drowned out by what was going on around me.

The triplets and Nicky were practicing this rap song they'd written.

"We're the rappin' Pikes, and we're here to say
We're hip, we're def, we're cool in every way
I'm Byron
I'm Adam
I'm Jordan
I'm Nick
For a real happenin' dude, just take your pick!"

Meanwhile, Vanessa, Claire, and Margo were playing a three-way game of "Miss Mary Mack" on the other side of the table. They clapped hands and then smacked them together patty-cake style, singing:

"Miss Mary Mack, Mack, Mack
All dressed in black, black, black
With silver buttons, buttons, buttons
All down her back, back, back."

Claire lagged behind on the words, since she was unsure of them, but she clapped hard and chimed in loudly on the last words of each line.

The noise was incredible. I looked at Mom and Dad, who would have ordinarily put a stop to the din long before it reached such an outrageous level. They seemed oblivious to the clamor. They were concentrating on their own conversation. In front of Mom was a piece of paper, and it looked like she was making a list. I strained to hear what my parents were saying.

"I think plain, bland foods would be best," said Dad. "You know, like chicken or fish."

"Right," said Mom. "Nothing too spicy or rich." She added to her list. "I'm sure I can come up with some menus he'll like."

Hmmm. I didn't think we'd be having tacos for dinner too often, not while Uncle Joe was with us. But I didn't mind. I knew that Mom was right about our having to make adjustments.

Meanwhile, the boys were still rapping, and the girls were still playing Miss Mary Mack. The two rhymes started to blend together:

"She asked her mother, mother, mother
For fifty cents, cents, cents
I'm a real jammin' dude and the girls agree
To see the elephants, elephants, elephants
There's no cooler guy than Jordan P.
Jump over the fence, fence, fence!"

I put my hands over my ears. "I can't take it anymore!" I yelled. "Mom, please tell them to stop."

She looked up at me, startled. "What, Mallory?" Then the noise seemed to register. She looked around the table. "Okay, that's enough," she said. "Time to settle down."

Nobody heard her. The rhymes continued:

"They jumped so high, high, high,
They touched the sky, sky, sky
So, hey, don't be jive
And they didn't come back, back, back
Give the Pike high five!
'Till the Fourth of July, July, July!"

The girls were clapping away, and the boys were giving each other their special high fives. They smacked each other's palms first, then the backs of their hands, then their palms again.

"Hey!" said Dad. "Yo!" *That* got their attention. "Time out," he said, making a T with his hands. "I know you're all excited about Uncle Joe coming. I am, too. But let's try to keep the noise down to a dull roar, okay? We're going to have to make an effort to be a little quieter while we have a visitor. We don't want to scare him off, do we?"

The kitchen grew silent.

"Sorry, Dad," said Vanessa in a small voice.

"Yeah, sorry," whispered Byron. "We'll be quiet when Uncle Joe gets here." He looked subdued.

"Well, you don't have to *whisper*," said Dad. "Uncle Joe knows he's coming to a house full of kids. He won't expect total silence."

Mom looked at her watch. "We'd better get going," she said. She looked over at me. "Are you sure you'll be okay on your own?"

I nodded. "No problem," I said. Usually when my parents go out they hire *two* sitters (I'm one of them, most of the time), since there are so many kids to watch. But today they'd only be gone for an hour or so, first to the supermarket and then to pick up Uncle Joe. Mom had agreed to let me sit alone.

Dad pushed his chair away from the table. "Okay, then," he said. "We'll be back soon. You guys will take care of this mess, right?" he asked, pointing at the breakfast dishes and now-empty cereal boxes.

"Don't worry, Dad," I said. "The house will be spotless by the time you get here with Uncle Joe."

As soon as my parents left, I began cleaning up the kitchen. I told the triplets to clear the table, and I told Margo and Claire to wipe it down. Vanessa and I rinsed the dishes, and Nicky put away the milk and peanut butter. The job was done in no time.

"*Now* can we tell?" I heard Claire whisper to Margo as I stood wiping my hands on a dishcloth.

"Okay," said Margo. "Hey everybody, want to see the surprise we made?" She didn't wait for an answer. She motioned to Claire, and they ran to their room. They came back a few minutes later carrying a huge length of computer paper. Then Margo took one end and Claire took the other, and they displayed the banner they'd made. WELKOME UNCLE JOW! it said. Flowers and rainbows decorated every corner, and each letter was a different color.

"Wow!" said Nicky. "That's neat!"

Margo and Claire grinned proudly.

"You spelled some stuff wrong," said Vanessa.

I saw Margo's face fall. "It doesn't matter," I said quickly. "Uncle Joe is going to be really, really impressed with that banner. It's beautiful." Actually, it was kind of a mess. I could see fingerprints in a few places, some of the flowers looked more like weird mushrooms, and several of the letters had big drips of paint running down them. But I knew that the girls had put a lot of time and effort into it, and I was sure Uncle Joe would be touched by their gesture. "I think we should hang it up on the front porch, where he'll see it right away," I said.

"I'll get a hammer," said Jordan.

"I'll get the stepladder," said Adam.

"I'll get some nails," said Byron. The triplets love to play "handyman."

"What can *I* do?" asked Nicky.

"You can help me make sure the banner is put up in the right place," I said. "And that it's not crooked."

We trooped out to the porch, and the triplets got to work. Nicky took his job seriously, offering suggestions and giving orders on how and where to hang the banner. Claire and Margo watched fearfully, worried that the banner would get torn. (Vanessa had gone to her room, saying that she wanted to write a poem for Uncle Joe.)

By the time we had hung the banner (it was still kind of crooked, even after Nicky had done his best to give directions), I was checking my watch every five seconds. I knew Mom and Dad would be home any minute, along with Uncle Joe.

I walked around the house, checking to make sure everything was neat. I opened the door of the den to see if Uncle Joe's room still looked cozy and welcoming. My sisters and brothers followed me. For once, they were pretty quiet. The house was as clean as it ever gets, so I decided we might as well relax. We were sitting in the living room when we finally heard a car pull into the driveway. "He's here!" yelled Nicky.

"Vanessa!" shouted Margo. "Uncle Joe's here!"

Vanessa flew down the stairs. "My poem's not done yet!" she gasped.

"Don't worry," I said. "He'll be here for a while. You can read it to him another time." We ran out the front door and stood on the porch, watching as first Dad, then Mom got out of the car. I could see a figure sitting in the backseat, but I couldn't make out his features. Dad opened the door for him, and Uncle Joe climbed out, stiffly and slowly. He held Dad's arm for balance. Then he and my parents turned and headed toward the house.

Uncle Joe was thin, and kind of bent over. His hair was white, and he wore little spectacles with wire rims. He had on a blue suit, and a starched white shirt buttoned up all the way to his neck. He wasn't wearing a tie, but he looked very dignified.

"Uncle Joe!" cried Claire. She ran down the steps and threw herself at him. He stepped back, looking alarmed. Dad caught Claire and held on to her.

"Gently, Claire," he said. "Take it easy. Uncle Joe, I'd like you to meet our youngest daughter, Claire."

Uncle Joe nodded stiffly, but didn't return the hug that Claire was trying to give him. "Hello," he said, in a dry, papery voice. He smiled thinly and patted Claire's head as if she were a dog.

"You're really my *great*-uncle," said Claire. "My great, wonderful, totally terrific uncle!"

Wow. Claire certainly was prepared to love Uncle Joe. And it was cute that she thought "great-uncle" meant that he was a great guy. But Uncle Joe didn't even seem to hear what she'd said. He gazed up at the rest of us, still standing on the porch, and frowned. It was as if he'd never seen a bunch of kids before.

"Come and meet the rest of the family," said Dad. He introduced us each in turn, and Uncle Joe nodded to us. He didn't seem interested in hugs or kisses.

"Oh, look at that!" said Mom, pointing at the banner and smiling. "Isn't that beautiful? I'll bet Margo and Claire made it."

They nodded. "It's for Uncle Joe," Claire pointed out.

Mom looked at Uncle Joe. "Did you see the banner?" she asked.

He glanced up at it. "Yes," he said shortly. "Very nice."

Claire and Margo looked a little stunned.

But Claire wasn't ready to give up. She grabbed Uncle Joe's hand and pulled him toward the door. "Come and see your room," she said. "We made it all ready for you."

Uncle Joe allowed himself to be led into the house, but as soon as he was inside the door he disengaged himself from Claire. Then he turned to Mom. "Would you be so kind as to show me to a sink?" he asked. "I'm afraid the child's hands are rather sticky."

I glanced at Claire's hands. They didn't seem any dirtier than usual, but maybe the Tootsie Pop she'd been eating earlier had made them a little sticky.

Mom showed Uncle Joe to the kitchen sink, and he scrubbed his hands for several minutes. The triplets watched with their mouths open.

Dad came up behind me. "Apparently he does this fairly often," he said quietly. "The nurses at Stoneybrook Manor mentioned that he can't stand dirt on his hands." Dad looked a little sad. I guess Uncle Joe wasn't living up to the character that Dad had remembered.

Uncle Joe wasn't telling funny stories, or pulling nickels out of people's ears. He wasn't warm or outgoing. In fact, he was pretty standoffish.

He hardly glanced at the room we'd spent so much time setting up for him; he just directed Byron to put his suitcase on the floor near the bed. Then he said he thought he'd take a short nap, and he closed the door.

We worked hard at keeping the house quiet while he slept. When he got up, he joined us in the living room. He still hadn't taken off his suit jacket and when he perched himself on the couch he didn't relax. He just sat there, bolt upright, frowning his little frown.

Soon Mom announced that dinner was ready. Uncle Joe followed us into the dining room and took his seat. Mom served up the food, and I was totally depressed when I saw what was on my plate. Chicken breast with no skin. Boiled potatoes. Cauliflower. No spices, no gravy, just a plate full of white foods. Yuck.

Uncle Joe ate carefully, taking small bites and chewing each one thoroughly. He didn't speak. And you know what? Nobody else did either. It must have been the first silent meal in the history of the Pikes.

We all went to bed early that night. The day we'd been waiting for had come and gone. How were we going to *stand* a whole month — or maybe longer — with Uncle Joe?

CHAPTER 6

I was happy to get out of the house for school on Monday morning. Uncle Joe was no more cheerful at breakfast than he'd been the day before. I thought about him on and off while I was in school. He seemed so withdrawn. He didn't seem to take much interest in his new surroundings. "I mean," I said to Jessi at lunch, "why did he want to visit us in the first place? He hasn't even bothered to learn our names." Jessi didn't have any answers.

After school, I headed for my job at the Craines'. I felt a little guilty about not going home, but to tell you the truth, I was secretly glad that I couldn't. Life was a lot more pleasant over at the Craine house, with no grouchy old Uncle Joe sitting around like a block of wood.

Sophie answered the door about two-and-a-half seconds after I'd rung the bell. "Mallory's here!" she yelled, giving me a huge grin. "Guess what?" she asked me.

"What?" I said, smiling back at her. It was nice to feel so welcomed.

"Aunt Bud's here!" she said.

Oh. Did that mean they didn't need me today? My smiled faded.

"Mommy's taking her to the doctor, but she came to our house for a visit first," continued Sophie.

Oh! That was better.

"Come on," said Sophie, pulling me by the hand. "Come and meet her."

I felt a little nervous as I followed Sophie into the kitchen. I'd never met a woman who rode a motorcycle before. She'd probably be wearing a leather jacket. What if she offered me a beer? I wondered if she had any tattoos.

"Hi," I heard as I walked into the kitchen. "You must be Mallory. The girls are already crazy about you!" The woman smiled at me. "I'm Ellen. Also known as Aunt Bud."

She was totally normal-looking, with curly brown hair and big blue eyes. No tattoos (at least none that I could see), no leather jacket, no beer can in her hand. She did, however, have a *huge* plaster cast on her right leg.

"Hi!" I said. "I'm crazy about the girls, too. I'm glad I got the chance to sit for them, but I'm sorry about your leg."

"Thanks," she said. "It's not so bad. I only have to wear this cast for another few weeks, and then the doctors said I'll have to take it easy for a while after that."

"Do you really have a motorcycle?" I asked.

"Yup," she said. "I just got it last year. It's a lot of fun, but you have to know what you're doing. I'm a pretty cautious rider."

I was about to ask if she would take me for a ride sometime after her leg was better (as if my parents would *ever* allow that), when Mrs. Craine came into the kitchen. "We'd better get going, Ell," she said. "Hi, Mallory," she went on, "thanks for being on time. Margaret will be getting home from school any minute, and Katie's due to wake up from her nap soon. I told Sophie that you could make cookies together today. I bought that slice-and-bake kind, and it's in the fridge."

"Great," I said. Sophie and I followed Mrs. Craine and Ellen as they headed for the door. "Um, Mrs. Craine," I said as she was slipping into her jacket. "I meant to ask you. Do you have a cat?"

"A cat?" she asked, looking perplexed. "No, no cat. Why?"

"I — I just wondered," I said.

She gave me a strange look, but she was in too much of a hurry to continue the conversation.

" 'Bye," said Ellen, as she limped out the door. "Nice meeting you, Mallory."

"Have fun," said Mrs. Craine, giving Sophie a quick hug. "See you in a few hours." Sophie and I watched as they drove away.

"Margaret *told* you we don't have a cat," she said to me.

"I know. I just wanted to double check." I felt bad that I hadn't believed the girls, but I just couldn't figure out what else could have been making that noise. "Hey," I said, glad to be able to change the subject, "there's Margaret's bus."

Margaret skipped up the front walk. "Hi, Mallory!" she shouted. "Look what I made!" She held up a homemade book tied with ribbon. "I'm an author!"

"Wow," I said. "Let's see." I paged through the book she handed me. It was a funny story about a little girl who becomes friends with a dinosaur. Her pictures were quite good. "Neat," I said.

"I know."

I love how kids don't pretend to be modest.

"Can I see?" asked Sophie.

"I'll read it to you later," said Margaret. Then she turned to me again. "We're learning about readers and writers in my class," she said. "Next week a really famous author is coming to talk to us."

"That's exciting," I said. "Why don't you come in and get changed, and then you can tell us about it while we make cookies."

"Cookies!" she yelled. "Yea!" She dashed past me and headed up to her room.

By the time Margaret was changed, Katie had woken up. She was a little cranky at first, but I held her and gave her a cup of juice, and soon she was smiling. "Okay," I said, "time to make cookies." I took the dough out of the fridge and turned on the oven. "Who knows where the cookie sheets are?" I asked.

"I do!" said Margaret. She opened a cabinet and pulled them out.

I set them out on the kitchen table. Then I put Katie in her high chair and sat the other two girls down next to her, Sophie in her booster seat and Margaret in a "grown-up" chair. I gave Margaret a butter knife, which I figured was too dull to hurt her, and let her cut up some of the dough. I cut the rest, and gave the pieces to Sophie and Katie. They arranged them on the cookie sheet.

"I'm going to make a big, giant one," said Sophie, sticking several pieces together.

Katie smooshed her piece around until it was kind of gray-looking, then carefully put it on the edge of the cookie sheet. She looked up at me and beamed.

"Good work," I said, even though the little

gray lump was basically disgusting.

"I'm going to make a snowman," said Margaret. She took three pieces of dough and started to arrange them on the sheet. Just then, I heard it. That mewing sound! And you know what? This time, the girls heard it, too. We stopped what we were doing and listened hard.

"Wow," said Margaret breathily. "That sure does sound like a cat."

"Kitty!" cried Katie.

"Let's find him," said Sophie.

"I bet he's under a bed or something," said Margaret.

"Find kitty," said Katie.

I turned off the oven and stuck the filled cookie sheets into the fridge. Obviously the cat was far more interesting than the cookies were, at least for the moment. "Okay," I said. "Let's start on this floor and work our way upstairs." I led the way. The search felt familiar, since I'd been through the same thing last time I was at the Craines'. But the girls knew about a few nooks and crannies I'd missed. Margaret showed me a little cubbyhole beneath the stairs, and Sophie pointed out a broom closet I hadn't noticed the other day.

But we couldn't find that cat.

The mewing continued as we searched. It

sounded very, very weak, like the cat was scared or hungry or sick or all three. I was really kind of worried about the cat.

We climbed to the second floor and looked some more. No cat.

"There's no cat anywhere!" said Margaret. "Maybe it's a *ghost* we're hearing. Maybe our house is haunted!"

"Shhh," I said. "You'll scare your sisters. Anyway, that's just plain silly. Whoever heard of a ghost cat? If we keep looking we'll find a real, live cat." I sounded sure of myself. But you know what? Margaret's idea had given me the shivers. That pitiful meowing was starting to get to me, and since we hadn't found even one cat *hair* the idea of a ghost didn't seem all that far off the mark.

Suddenly I noticed that the room we were standing in was kind of dim. The afternoon had flown by, and it was beginning to grow dark outside. I switched on the light. I felt spooked enough; I didn't need to be walking around in a pitch-black house. We were in Margaret's room, and I sat down on her bed with the girls. We could still hear meowing and, as a matter of fact, it sounded louder on the second floor than it had on the first.

"Okay," I said. "Let's make a plan. We know that we want to find that cat. We've looked downstairs and we've looked upstairs, and we still haven't found it. Right?"

The girls nodded. They looked very serious. They were really caught up in this cat hunt.

"So," I continued, "we need to figure out where we haven't looked. Can anybody remember if there's somewhere we *haven't* looked?"

Silence.

"In the attic," Margaret whispered, after a short pause.

"What?"

"The attic. We haven't gone up there."

"Well, now we're going to," I said, trying to sound brave. "I — I mean, are you allowed up there?"

"As long as a grown-up is with us, we are," answered Margaret.

I figured I probably qualified as a grown-up in this case.

"We need a flashlight," said Margaret. "There are no lights up there."

We rounded up a flashlight and then we headed for the attic door. I turned the key that was in the lock, and door swung open. I carried Katie up the steep stairs, following Margaret and Sophie, who led the way. The attic was warm and it smelled musty. I happen to like that smell, so I closed my eyes and took a deep sniff. "Whoops!" I said, as I nearly tripped over an old trunk. I put Katie down and shone my flashlight around the little room. I saw angled walls, one tiny window, and a lot of boxes and old furniture. "Wow," I said. "There's a lot of stuff up here."

"Most of it was here when we moved to the house," said Margaret. "Daddy keeps saying he's going to clean it out, but he never has time."

I looked closer at the three-legged table that was propped against a box. "This looks really old," I said. "Too bad its missing a — "

Just then, I saw a streak of white fly out from under the table.

Sophie shrieked. Katie looked surprised and sat down suddenly. Margaret's eyes grew wide. "A cat!" she said. She took off after it. It ran around the attic twice before it spotted the stairs. Then it flew down the steps, with Margaret close on its heels. I followed, carrying Katie and holding Sophie's hand.

"Down here!" shouted Margaret from the first floor. "Quick!"

I hurried down the stairs with the other two girls, and found Margaret standing outside the laundry room. The door was closed.

"He went in here," she said, "I caught him."

I opened the door a crack and peeked inside. "He looks scared," I said. It was a small, white cat with huge round eyes that almost looked silver. He gazed at me from the corner where he'd hidden. I felt a little shiver run down my spine.

The girls pushed near me so that they could peek, too. "Hi, ghost cat," said Margaret. "It's okay, we won't hurt you."

"Ghost Cat," I said. "That'a good name for him, don't you think?" The girls nodded.

"Maybe he's hungry," said Sophie.

"Cookie!" said Katie.

"Well, I don't think he'd like a cookie so much," I said. "But let's see what else we have to give him." I closed the door carefully. We trooped into the kitchen, and I found some cold chicken in the fridge. I shredded it into a bowl, filled another bowl with water, and headed back to the laundry room. I opened the door, shoved the bowls inside, and closed the door quickly.

"I wonder where he was hiding up there?" I said. "And how did he get in and out?"

"Let's go look," said Margaret.

So we headed back up to the attic. I shone my flashlight around until I found an opening in the rafters that led outside. "He could have come in through there," I said. "If he climbed that big tree by the living room window, he'd be able to reach the roof."

"I guess he liked our attic because it's all warm and cozy," said Margaret. "And because there're no dogs or anything in here."

"Right," I said. "He must have stayed alive by eating mice and things that he caught outside."

"Ew!" said Sophie.

"Well, cats like mice the way you like cookies," I said smiling. "And, speaking of cookies, why don't we finish our baking before your mom gets home? Then you can have cookies for dessert tonight."

When Mrs. Craine returned, the girls were eager for her to meet Ghost Cat. "Can we keep him?" begged Margaret.

"Please?" added Sophie.

"Keep kitty?" asked Katie.

"I guess it's okay," said Mrs. Craine, "since he already seems to live here. We should take him to the vet, and make sure he's had all his shots. But first we should make sure he doesn't belong to anybody else."

"You could put an ad in the *Stoneybrook News*," I said. "That way, if nobody claims him, you'll know he's probably just a stray."

Mrs. Craine seemed to like that idea, and as I left that afternoon, she and the girls were already hard at work composing the ad.

CHAPTER 7

Fryday

Wow. Today I missed Mimi more than ever. I had forggoten what its' like to be around an old persson, but being with Mal's Unckle Joe reminded me. Except that Unckle Joe isnt' anything like Mimi. And that's what reely made me miss her. She was always so warm and she made me feel speshall. On the other hand, Unckle Joe made me feel like two cents.

MY parents had tickets to a concert that Friday night. Since every single one of my brothers and sisters was going to be home, Mom had hired Claudia to come over and be my co-babysitter. Claudia was interested in the "new" person in our household, so she was looking forward to the job. But, as she wrote in the club notebook, meeting Uncle Joe did *not* turn out to be such a pleasure.

I think Claud's mind was on Mimi before she even got to our house that night. Mimi was Claudia's grandmother, and she lived with the Kishis until she died. It hasn't been that long since Claud lost Mimi, and I think the pain is still pretty sharp. Mimi was the greatest. She had this presence that I can only describe as *serene*. Do you know what that means? I looked it up in the dictionary once, just because I liked the sound of the word. "Serene," it said. "Unruffled; tranquil; dignified." That describes Mimi, for sure. No wonder Claud loved her so much.

Mimi did have her ups and downs though, especially after she had her stroke. She'd forget things, or act cranky, or think people were out to get her. But you know what? I hate to say it, but even at her worst, she was better than Uncle Joe.

I could see that Claudia was a little taken aback when she first met Uncle Joe that night. She was probably expecting the warm, jovial guy my father had told us about. I'd repeated some of his stories during club meetings (*before* Uncle Joe came) and so far I hadn't been able to bring myself to tell everybody the truth about what he was *really* like.

"Hi!" Claudia said brightly, when she found Joe sitting in the living room. "You must be Uncle Joe. I'm Claudia." She stuck out her hand to shake his.

I saw him wince a little. "My name is Mr. Pike," he said, without smiling. He shook her hand gingerly, then pulled his back and examined it as if he were worried that she'd dirtied it.

Claudia blushed. "I — I'm sorry," she said. "I didn't mean to — "

He waved his hand, impatient with her stammering. "Young people," he muttered. "No respect for their elders." He didn't seem to be talking to Claudia — it was more like he was just talking to himself.

Claudia looked as if she were in shock. I pulled her into the kitchen. "Don't mind him," I said. "He's just — "

"He's just a mean old man!" she burst out. Then she covered her mouth with her hand.

"I'm sorry, Mal," she said. "I really didn't mean it. I was just surprised. I'm sure he's a nice person."

"I wouldn't be so sure," I muttered. But I let the matter drop, since my parents were on their way out the door and it was time for Claud and me to start getting dinner ready.

"So," said Claud, rubbing her hands together once we were alone in the kitchen, "what's being served at the Pike residence tonight?" She gave me a mischievous grin. "Fried bologna-and-sardine sandwiches? Cheez-it omelets? Spaghetti with chocolate sauce?"

Claudia likes to make fun of the way we eat.

"Sorry, Claud," I said, giving her a shrug. "Tonight's menu is a little less exotic. How does this sound?" I ticked off the items. "Brussels sprouts, mashed turnips, white rice with no butter, and well-done minute steaks."

"Ew!" said Claud. "Come on, what's *really* for dinner?"

"I'm not making it up," I said. "That's how we've been eating all week. Mom says she lies in bed at night, staring at the ceiling and trying to come up with bland menus for Uncle Joe."

"He *likes* that kind of food?" asked Claud.

"Well, I'm not sure," I answered. "He doesn't say a word one way or the other. He never compliments Mom on her cooking, but he never complains, either. So who knows what he thinks?"

"Boy," said Claudia. "I bet I know what the *rest* of you think of having to eat that way!"

I nodded. "Everybody's really trying hard to make this visit work out," I said. "But it hasn't been easy."

We worked quietly together in the kitchen, and when dinner was ready Claud rounded everybody up. She called, "Dinner's ready!" and the triplets slid down the banister, one after the other. They were carrying that week's favorite toy — laser guns — and pretending to blast away at any object in their path. Nicky ran down the stairs after them, shouting at them to wait up. Vanessa and Margo had been doing their homework in the rec room, but they were glad to put it away. And Claire showed up in a pair of Mom's old high heels and a "fur stole" Mom had made for her out of an old fuzzy bedspread.

Uncle Joe came into the dining room last. He walked stiffly, as if he weren't used to moving his arms and legs too much. He looked around at us and gave a small smile. "Good evening," he said, nodding slightly at Claud. He looked as if he had no idea who she was. It was almost as if he didn't remember meeting her just half an hour earlier. Then he pulled out his chair, sat down, and folded his hands in his lap.

Claud looked over at me. I shrugged. Then I made up a plate of food for Uncle Joe and set it at his place. He didn't thank me, and he didn't wait for anyone else to be served. He just picked up his fork and began to eat, very neatly and very steadily. He took tiny bites and chewed each one thoroughly. He didn't say a word.

The rest of us were pretty quiet, too. Nobody looked too enthusiastic about the food. In fact, nobody was really eating it. Nicky was pushing a Brussels sprout around his plate, trying to hide it under the mashed turnips. I saw Adam look at his gray steak with a disgusted grimace. Claire was taking tiny sips of milk from her glass and ignoring her food completely.

Suddenly Margo squealed, "Cut that *out!*"

"Shhh, Margo," I said. "We're at the dinner table, remember?" I gave her a Look, nodding my head toward Uncle Joe. Mom and Dad had asked us to try extra-hard to keep mealtimes "civil" as long as he was visiting.

"I *know* we're at the dinner table," she said, glaring back at me. "But Nicky keeps pinching me. And a second ago, he stole my shoe right off my foot!"

"Nicky," I said, focusing my Look on him, "is that true?"

Nicky ignored the question. Instead, he whispered something to Jordan, who was sitting on his other side. Jordan gave a sudden laugh, and a few grains of rice flew out of his mouth. They landed a foot or so from Uncle Joe's plate.

Uncle Joe stood up. "I've had about as much of this tomfoolery as I can take!" he said. He turned and left the room.

The rest of us watched him march away. We were in shock. At least *I* was. What Uncle Joe had just blown up at was about one one-*hundredth* of what normally goes on at our dinner table. Claudia looked over at me. "Wow," she said, under her breath. "He's a little *touchy*, wouldn't you say?"

"Touchy?" I asked with a straight face. "What in the world makes you say that?" Then I burst into giggles. And every one of my brothers and sisters followed my example. At first I tried to stifle my laughter, but after a few seconds, I gave up. It felt so good to laugh!

Then I picked up my plate. "Anybody for sardines?" I asked. Everybody else picked up their plates and fell into line behind me as I marched into the kitchen. I threw open the refrigerator door. "Help yourselves!" I said. I put my plate on the counter. Later, I'd make sure that none of that bland, yucky food went to waste. Maybe Mom could make some kind of casserole out of the leftovers. But for now, I was dying for something with some *taste* to it, and I was sure everyone else was, too.

"Are you sure this is okay?" Claudia asked me.

"I'm sure," I said. "I know Mom won't blame us for anything. Now, let's eat some *real* food!" I grabbed a jar of salsa, a brick of cheese, and some flour burritos from the fridge. "I'll make you a Mallory Special," I told Claud.

Once everyone had found what they wanted to eat, we hung out in the kitchen, munching away and laughing together. I'd almost managed to forget about Uncle Joe when Margo spoke up.

"Why is Uncle Joe so sad?" she asked. "I feel sorry for him. I wish we could help him feel better."

I couldn't think of a thing to say. I felt ashamed that my little sister's attitude was so much more sensitive than mine. Here I was, first feeling impatient with Uncle Joe and then practically forgetting he existed. And here was Margo, wishing she could cheer him up.

"It's hard being old," explained Claudia. "Even Mimi got cranky sometimes. When you're old, your body can feel stiff and achy.

You can't concentrate on things so well, and sometimes you get confused. You like to have things a certain way, and changes can upset you."

Wow. All of a sudden I saw things from Uncle Joe's perspective. I'd been thinking about me and my family, and how hard it was to have him for a visitor. But now I realized it must be difficult for him, too. We *are* a pretty rowdy crew.

"So what can we do?" I asked Claudia. Since she lived with Mimi for so long, I figured she must be an expert on having an older person in your house.

"I think he just needs time to get used to you," she said. "And I think you need to give him a chance to adjust. You don't have to act like perfect children. That wouldn't be right for you, either. But try not to take it personally when he has a hard time dealing with life in the Pike household."

Claire and Margo had been whispering in the corner while Claud was talking. "We have an idea!" said Claire. "We're going to bring Uncle Joe a piece of cake for dessert, and then perform our play for him. Maybe that will cheer him up."

I looked at Claudia. She shrugged and nodded. "Can't hurt," she said.

"Okay," I agreed. I'd seen the "play" before, so I knew what Uncle Joe was in for. It was a mishmash of fairy tales: Little Red Riding Hood meets Snow White while walking through the woods to Hansel and Gretel's house. Margo and Claire each played several parts.

I cut a piece of cake and put it on a plate. I gave it to Claire to carry, and I handed Margo a glass of milk to go with it. I followed them into the living room, where Uncle Joe was once again slumped in "his" chair.

"We brought you something," said Claire.

"What?" asked Uncle Joe. The girls had startled him.

"Want some cake?" asked Margo. "And milk?" She handed him the glass, and Claire gave him the plate. He accepted them both without saying anything. He wasn't frowning, though. I thought I saw a smile. "Now we're going to do our play for you," said Margo. "You're the audience, okay?"

Uncle Joe sighed. He looked like he just wanted to be left alone. "To be frank — " he began.

"Okay, ready?" said Margo to Claire. They dashed downstairs to the toy chest in the rec room and got out their "costumes" (mainly kerchiefs and aprons) and props (a large picnic basket was the main one). Then the play began.

I didn't hold out much hope for Claire and Margo's plan. I headed back to the kitchen, where Claudia was trying to trick the triplets, Nicky, and Vanessa into cleaning up.

"Thanks for your advice," I said. "I mean, about living with old people. I really *do* want Uncle Joe to enjoy his visit here. And I'll work harder at being patient."

Claudia smiled at me. "I know it isn't easy," she said. "But I think it might be worth the effort if you can hang in there."

When the kitchen was clean, Claudia and I tiptoed back to the living room to check on Claire, Margo, and Uncle Joe. We peeked into the room, and then pulled back with our hands over our mouths to quiet our giggles.

Claire and Margo were still busily involved in acting out their complicated story. They hadn't even noticed that Uncle Joe had dozed off. He sat in the chair with his chin on his chest, sleeping peacefully, as they pranced around the room in their costumes.

I shook my head. "Oh, well," I said.

Then Claudia pointed out something that made me feel that Claire and Margo had made a *little* progress.

"Look," she said, pointing to the arm of Uncle Joe's chair. There sat an empty plate, an empty glass beside it. "At least he ate the cake!"

CHAPTER 8

I'd begun to look forward to each of my sitting jobs with the Craine girls. Margaret, Sophie, and Katie are three of the sweetest girls I've ever known. Also, I hate to admit it, but it was a relief to get out of the house and away from Uncle Joe and his cloud of bad feelings a few times a week. Actually, I felt a little guilty about abandoning the rest of my family so often, but Mom and Dad assured me it was okay with them. Since Uncle Joe spent an awful lot of his time just dozing or sitting quietly in his chair, it wasn't as if he *missed* me when I was gone.

Anyway, I must confess that I usually forgot about Uncle Joe the second I walked into the Craines' house. There was always a lot going on, and the girls demanded my full attention.

That Tuesday was no different. When I let myself in (Mrs. Craine had told me not to bother knocking, since I was expected) I heard shrieks of laughter coming from the living room. And when I popped my head around the corner and said "Hi!", the girls mobbed me.

"MalloryBalloryTallory!" yelled Sophie.

"Guess what, Mallory?" shouted Margaret.

"HiHiHiHiHi!" said Katie, with a huge grin.

"Hi, girls," I said, laughing. "It's good to see you."

"Guess what?" asked Margaret again.

"What?" I asked.

"We're doing a play!" chorused the girls.

Oh no, another play. Didn't I get enough of this at home? I resisted the impulse to sigh and roll my eyes. "Great!" I said, trying to sound sincere. "Who's in it?"

"All our babies," said Sophie. "It's a play about a lady with a million babies."

Katie approached me with an armful of dolls. She began to arrange them on my lap, telling me their names as she posed them. "Barbie B.," she said, sitting a Barbie on my right thigh. "Nancy," she said, as she tucked a baby doll into my arms. "Martha," she said, showing me a floppy rag doll.

"I'm glad to meet all your babies," I said, trying to contain my giggles.

Mrs. Craine walked into the living room then, buttoning up her coat. "Isn't it something how she comes up with those names?"

she said. "I don't know how she thinks of them, but the second she gets a new doll, she has a name for it." She gave each of the girls a quick hug. "I'm on my way," she said. "Have fun!"

"I don't *want* you to leave!" said Sophie suddenly. She threw her arms around her mother's knees.

I was surprised. That had never happened before. I looked at Mrs. Craine.

"She's a little sleepy, I think," she said. "She only had a short nap this afternoon." She looked down at her daughter. Sophie was frowning and holding on tight. "Honey," she said. "I have to go. But I'll be back soon. And you'll have a good time with Mallory."

Sophie shook her head and readjusted her grip. "I want to go *with* you," she whined.

It was time for the oldest trick in the baby-sitters' book. "Sophie," I said. "I brought some special toys for you to play with today. Toys you've never even seen before!" I went to the hall table where I'd left my Kid-Kit when I came in. I held up the box so Sophie could see it. Immediately she let go of her mother and ran to my side. Mrs. Craine smiled at me and waved good-bye as she tiptoed out the door.

Distraction. It rarely fails.

Sophie took the box from me and sat on the

floor with it, rummaging through the stuff inside. Kid-Kits are great. I've never seen a kid who could resist them. They were another of Kristy's ideas for our club. They're just boxes that we've decorated so that they look kind of fancy, and then filled with little toys, games, books, stickers, crayons. You name it, it's in there. Not all of the stuff is new. I get a lot of cast-off toys from my brothers and sisters for my Kid-Kit, but since the things are new to the kids we sit for, they find them fascinating.

Katie and Margaret joined Sophie on the floor. I have toys in my kit for all different age levels, so each girl found something to play with, and there wasn't much squabbling. Their play was forgotten, and I can't say I minded.

"I love this book, Mallory," said Margaret. She was looking at a tiny paperback copy of *Angelina Ballerina.* "Can I keep it?"

I could tell that she longed to own that book. "I can't let you keep it," I said, "because I baby-sit for a lot of kids who love it, too." Margaret's face fell. "But I promise to bring it with me every time I come." Margaret cheered up. I knew I'd have to tell Mrs. Craine that the book had been a hit. Maybe Margaret would get it for her next birthday.

Katie was playing with a small stuffed elephant she'd found at the bottom of the box. "Bobby," she said, naming him.

"Okay," I said. "Bobby it is. Bobby the Elephant. He never even *had* a name before, and now he has the perfect one." Katie beamed.

Sophie was trying on a sequined tiara, one of the most popular items in my kit. "I'm a princess," she said. "Princess Aurora." She began to spin around in the middle of the room.

Just then I heard a meow. "Ghost Cat!" I said. I'd almost forgotten about him. "How's he doing?"

"He's fine," said Margaret, putting down the book. "Want to see him?" She led the way to the laundry room. But she stopped suddenly and put her hand over her mouth. "I forgot," she said. "He always runs out when we open the door. Then we have to look all over the house and find him and catch him."

"Well, maybe we better just leave him alone," I said.

"No, no!" said Sophie. "I want to show him to you."

"Show cat!" said Katie.

Margaret looked torn. But her pride as a new pet owner won out. "He's so pretty," she said. "He's gotten fatter and shinier since we've been taking care of him. I'll open the door just a little bit, and you can peek inside really fast, okay?"

"Okay," I said. "If you're sure . . ."

Margaret opened the door — just a crack — and Ghost Cat *shot* out of the laundry room. "Oh!" she said, watching him go. There was no point in chasing him; he was moving too fast. "He'll go hide somewhere now, and then we can find him," she said.

We waited for a few minutes. Then we started to search the house, whistling and calling. "Heeeeere, kittykittykitty!" I called.

"Come here, Ghost Cat," said Margaret. "I have a treat for you!" She'd picked up a little box of cat treats, and she was shaking it to make a rattling noise. "Sometimes he hears this and he comes to me," she explained.

But Ghost Cat didn't fall for the old "treats" trick. He stayed hidden. We looked *everywhere* — under beds, in closets, even under the refrigerator. No Ghost Cat.

"I know! I bet he's in the attic," said Sophie. "I'll get my flashlight and we can look."

I'd noticed that the door to the attic was shut, so I knew there was no way he could be in there, but I didn't want to make Sophie feel bad by ignoring her suggestion.

Armed with flashlights, we climbed the stairs one more time. "Here, kittykittykitty," I called. I shone my light around the room. Did I mention before that I love attics? There's nothing I like better than poking through a bunch of musty, dusty old stuff, looking for forgotten treasures. Old clothes, ancient pictures, antique furniture; these things make history come to life for me. Of course, this attic wasn't *my* attic, so I didn't feel that I could explore it fully. But I couldn't resist taking a quick peek around while the girls checked every corner for Ghost Cat.

I saw an old dressmaker's dummy, standing silently in a corner. The woman who'd used it must have been *tiny*. The waist looked so small I bet I could have put my two hands around it. An old hat with faded red roses spilling off the sides was on the dummy's head. A bookshelf stood nearby, full of dusty old books with leather bindings and gold writing on their spines. My hands itched to hold them, but I held myself back.

Finally I said, "I don't think we're going to find him up here, girls. Why don't we go back downstairs and have a snack while we figure out what to do next?" Margaret and Sophie looked reluctant about leaving the attic without Ghost Cat, but Katie's eyes lit up when she heard the word "snack."

"Apple juice?" she asked. "Cracker?"

I picked her up and started for the stairs with the other girls following behind me. My flashlight beam hit something I hadn't seen before. "An old hat box!" I said. "Oh, how neat. I wonder if there's a hat inside it?" The round box was striped in faded pink and white, and the carrying handle was of braided pink silk. I put Katie down and gently opened the box. And what was inside was much, much better than a hat.

"Letters!" said Margaret.

"Lots of letters!" said Sophie.

I picked up the bundle of letters that was tied with a blue ribbon, and shone my flashlight on them. The envelopes were yellowed and crumbling, and the handwriting on the front of the top one was pale and spidery. "Wow," I said. "These are really, really old."

"Let's take them downstairs and read them!" said Margaret.

She didn't have to twist *my* arm. "Okay," I said. "Let's go!"

Under the bright lights of the kitchen, the writing on the envelopes was easier to read. The letters were all addressed to a Samuel K. Graham, and the return addresses read "Kennedy Graham, 94 High St." That was the Craines' address! As I sifted through the packet, a note — not in an envelope — fell out from between two letters. *"Abigail,"* it said (I read it out loud to the girls), *"I thought you'd like to have our Uncle Kennedy's letters, since you are now living in what used to be his house. Regards, your cousin Samuel."*

"Okay," I said, beginning to put the picture

together. "This man Kennedy Graham lived in this house a long, long time ago. And when he was living here, he wrote these letters to his nephew. Then, a long time later, a niece of his, Abigail, ended up living here. And Samuel sent her the letters."

"Neat!" said Margaret. "So the letters might have stuff about our house in them!"

"Right," I said. "Do you want to read one?"

Margaret nodded eagerly, but when she shook one of the letters out of its envelope and began to examine it closely, she realized the old-fashioned handwriting was too hard for her to read. "I can't do it," she said, sounding frustrated. "He made his letters too funny."

"How about if I read?" I asked. "Then we can all hear at once." Margaret handed me the letter and I began to read. *"Dear Samuel,"* the letter said. *"Weather today is clear and bright. I have seen a number of robins on the front lawn, which tells me that spring is surely here. A visitor arrived on my doorstep this morning: a small, sickly, white kitten."*

"A kitten!" cried Margaret. I smiled at her and went on reading.

"As I am without human companionship, I have taken the cat in and vowed to care for it."

That letter went on with some kind of boring details about a root cellar that Kennedy Graham was planning to dig that summer. I put it down and picked up the next one, which was dated a few months later. *"Dear Samuel,"* I read. The girls were staring at me with round eyes, eager to hear more about the kitten. *"The leaves have begun to turn scarlet and gold, and Tinker (that is the name I have given my tomcat) chases each and every one as it falls. He has grown into a fine, sleek animal, and he is my dearest friend."*

Margaret clapped her hands. "More!" she said. Sophie jumped up and down. Katie, who probably didn't understand too much, just grinned. I went on reading. The letters were really interesting, but the best parts were about the cat. Apparently Kennedy Graham had been really, really lonely before the cat came to live with him. He loved that cat and I could tell he spoiled it rotten. *"Tinker had chicken livers for his supper tonight, as I had roasted one of my best hens for myself. He loved the taste and ate until he could barely move . . ."*

I was getting to like Kennedy Graham, and Tinker, too. So it was a shock to read that the cat had died *". . . of a wasting disease that left him thin as a rail before it took his life."* I could see that the girls were upset by the cat's death, so I tried to screen the rest of the letters as I read them. It was sad. After the cat died, Kennedy Graham was never the same again. He was *"distraught . . ."* He constantly thought he heard the cat meowing, *"crying as if his heart had broken . . ."* — and the sound seemed to come from the attic!

I got a chill when I read that. *Had* the ghost of Tinker come back to be with Kennedy Graham? Or had Kennedy Graham gone a little crazy?

"He *looks* kind of weird," said Margaret, picking up an old, fuzzy photo that had fallen out of one of the letters. She showed it to me. Kennedy Graham had been a craggy, white-haired man with a small scar under his left eye. "A cat scratch, I bet!" said Margaret, looking at it.

Just as she said that, I heard a meow. Loudly. And the sound was coming from upstairs! I swear, the hair on the back of my neck stood up. But I gathered my courage and ran upstairs to check the attic. Maybe it was our own Ghost Cat, stuck up there after all.

There was no cat in the attic. But here's the *weird* thing. Right after I went to the attic, I checked the laundry room. And there was Ghost Cat, curled up cozily on top of some clean towels. He'd been there all along.

Friday

Cats, cats, cats. Has the world gone cat-crazy? First it's Mallory and the Ghost Cat over at the Craines; then it's those old letters about, what else, a cat. Then, just when I think I've heard as much about cats as I can stand, I sit at the Kormans' and Melody herself turns into a cat. Did you guys ever hear people talk about "dog people" and "cat people"? Well, I've decided I am a dog person. I have no use for cats. Please, Mary Anne, don't get upset — I still like Tigger — but only because he's a quiet cat. I never want to hear another "meow" as long as I live!

Kristy was sitting for the three Korman kids that evening. The Kormans have become pretty regular clients since they moved into Kristy's neighborhood, and Kristy sits for them more than the rest of us do because she lives across the street from them.

The evening had started off well. Kristy had made special arrangements to bring her stepsister Karen along with her, since Karen and Melody are the same age (seven) and have become good friends. When Kristy and Karen arrived at the Kormans' door, Melody threw it open before they could even ring the bell.

"I saw you coming up the walk!" she said. "I am so, so happy you're here."

"Well, I'm glad to *be* here," said Kristy, smiling.

"Not *you*, silly!" said Melody. Kristy's face fell. "I mean," said Melody, realizing she might have hurt Kristy's feelings, "I'm glad to see you, but I'm *really* glad to see Karen. Skylar's asleep and Bill is being *so* boring. All he wants to do is line up his G.I. Joes and talk about which weapons each one knows how to use. Yucko."

"Yucko," echoed Karen.

"So now that you're here, we can play!" said Melody to Karen. "What should we do first?"

"Let's pretend that we're mermaids and the

fountain is our swimming pool!" said Karen.

Yes, there's a fountain in the Kormans' front hall! Remember I told you that Kristy lives in a mansion? Well, most of the other houses in her neighborhood are mansion-type houses, too. And the Kormans' is the most mansion-like of all. But there's one thing I should mention about the fountain, which, by the way, is shaped like a fish standing on its tail. When the Kormans moved into this house, not too long ago, they thought the fountain was kind of funny, so they turned it on. Skylar panicked! She's only a year old, and I can't even begin to imagine why that fountain scared her so much, but it did. So the Kormans turned the fountain off, and it's stayed off.

I like the fact that the Kormans thought the fountain was silly, and didn't mind turning it off. The family that lived in that house before — the Delaneys — were really kind of stuck up. *They* thought the fountain was "elegant," and the kids boasted about it, along with the swimming pool, the *two* tennis courts, and all the other features of the house.

Anyway, after Mr. and Mrs. Korman had left, Melody didn't want to play in the fountain that night. "I'm tired of being mermaids," she said. "Let's do something else."

"How about a game of 'Let's All Come In'?" asked Karen, hopefully. That's her favorite game, probably because she invented it. It's a "let's pretend" game about various guests checking into a fancy old hotel.

"Nah," said Melody. "Not enough people. Bill won't play, and Skylar's too young to play, even if she was awake, and if it's just you and me it's no fun."

Kristy was kind of relieved. Let's All Come In isn't necessarily one of *her* favorite games. Somehow it often seems to cause bickering among the players. Everybody always wants to play the fun characters — the wealthy guests — and nobody wants to play the boring parts, like the bellhop.

"I guess you're right," Karen said to Melody. "Hmmmm . . . Oh! I know!" she said. "How about Lovely Ladies? We haven't played that in a long, long time."

Kristy thought they'd played Lovely Ladies just the week before, but she didn't say anything. And if Melody remembered, she didn't seem to mind. "Yea!" she said. "Lovely Ladies! I got the neatest new hat from Mommy. Come on, I'll show you."

They ran upstairs to Melody's room. Lovely Ladies is a dress-up game that Amanda Delaney, who was one of Karen's best friends before she moved away, had made up. Kristy knew the girls would be occupied for a while, so she decided to look in on Bill. She poked her head into his room. "Hiya!" she said. "What's up?"

Bill was lying on his back on the rag rug in the middle of the floor. He was holding a toy helicopter in one hand, and a toy jet in the other. "Pow!" he said. "Blam-blam-blam-BLAM!" He waved his arms around so that the jet and the helicopter seemed to be involved in an air battle. He was in another world; Kristy knew he hadn't even heard her.

"Bill!" she said, more loudly. "Yo!"

Bill stopped making noises for a second and looked over at her. "Oh, hi!" he said. He raised his eyebrows, as if he were wondering what she wanted from him.

"I just stopped in to see how you're doing," explained Kristy.

"I'm okay," he said, quickly. He obviously wanted to be left alone to finish off his dogfight.

"Okay," said Kristy. She started to leave Bill's room, but then she stuck her head back in at the last minute. "We'll be having dinner soon," she said.

Bill was already making explosion noises again. He nodded at her without interrupting his battle.

Kristy shrugged and headed down the hall to Skylar's room. "Banky!" she heard, just as she opened the door. Skylar had woken up from her nap. And she wanted her blanket, which she'd thrown out of her crib. Kristy bent down and picked it up.

"Here's your banky," she said. Then she held out her arms. "Ready to get up?" she asked. Skylar's usually a pretty happy baby. She gave Kristy a big grin. Kristy lifted her out of the crib, changed her diaper (babies are almost *always* wet — or worse — when they wake up from a nap), and dressed her in a clean romper.

"Let's go find your brother and sister and *my* stepsister and then we'll make dinner," she said, as she bounced Skylar on her hip. "How does that sound?"

Skylar smiled and clapped her hand together. "Eat!" she said.

"That's right," said Kristy. "Eat." She carried Skylar down the hall to Melody's room. By that time, Melody and Karen were heavily involved in their Lovely Ladies game. Melody was wearing a pink tutu, silver high-heeled shoes, a wedding veil, and a "diamond" necklace. Karen was wearing a long red cloak with a hood (usually used for putting on plays with Little Red Riding Hood as a character), and she was carrying a magic wand. At the top of the wand was a pink star with sequins on it, and pink and purple streamers.

"Oh," said Melody, looking at herself in the mirror, "I am a lovely, lovely lady."

Kristy had to stifle a giggle. She knew that this was the most important part of the game, and the dialogue was always the same. She mouthed Karen's line along with her.

"Would you like to have some tea?" asked Karen, who was also painstakingly admiring her reflection.

"Why certainly," said Melody. "Lovely Ladies must always have tea."

That's about the extent of the Lovely Ladies game!

Kristy applauded, which was kind of awkward, since she was still carrying Skylar. "Very nice outfits, girls!" she said. "Now, are you Lovely Ladies ready for dinner?"

"Almost," said Karen. "First we have to say our lines over again, but this time *I* go first." She turned to Melody. "Oh-I-am-a-lovely-lovely-lady," she said quickly. They ran the little scene over again in a flash.

"Okay," said Kristy. "Who wants to help make dinner?"

"I do!" called Karen. She loves to help in the kitchen.

"Meow!" said Melody.

"*What?*" asked Kristy.

"Meow," repeated Melody. She was busy

taking off her Lovely Lady outfit. "I'm tired of being a lovely lady. From now on I'm going to be a cat."

"Tat!" said Skylar, with a fearful look on her face.

"Don't worry, Skylar," said Melody. "I'm not the kind of cat you're scared of. I'm a *Melody*-cat!"

Kristy remembered then that Skylar has a terrible fear of cats. But the baby seemed reassured by her sister's statement. "Melody-tat!" said Skylar, smiling. *"Pat* Melody-tat!" She struggled to get out of Kristy's arms and began to stroke Melody's head.

"Purr, purr," said Melody.

"Cats are kind of boring," said Karen suddenly. She adjusted her cloak. "Don't you at least want to be a Lovely Lady at the dinner table?" she asked Melody. Karen can be bossy sometimes, and once in a while when some *other* kid comes up with a good idea, Karen will resist it. She wants to be the one running the show.

"Meow," said Melody, sinking even further into her cat role. Melody loves to play pretend. She rubbed her head against Kristy's leg and ignored Karen.

Kristy looked at Karen and shrugged. "Oh well," she said. "I guess we'll have dinner with one baby, one boy, one Lovely Lady, and one cat."

Karen pouted, but she followed Kristy, who was carrying Skylar again, and Melody (who was padding along on tiptoe with her "paws" held out in front of her) to the kitchen. Karen helped Kristy set the table, while Melody pretended to play with a piece of string. Then Karen helped Kristy make a salad, while Melody pretended to drink from a bowl of milk that Kristy had poured for the "cat." And when dinner was ready, Karen ran to get Bill, while Melody took a "catnap" under the table.

"What's for dinner?" asked Bill. "Hot dogs, I bet. That's what we *always* have when baby-sitters are here."

"Well, I fooled you this time," said Kristy. "How do fishsticks sound, instead?"

"Yea!" said Bill. "I love them. So does Skylar. Melody doesn't like them so much, though."

It was a good thing Bill and Skylar were happy with the meal, since Karen and Melody were pretty glum. Karen was clearly having a hard time dealing with Melody's cat act, and Melody was having a hard time with the fishsticks. Kristy decided just to let Melody pick at her bun, as long as she ate a little salad. And as for Karen, Kristy decided that it would be best if she headed home soon after dinner.

"I'm going to call your mom and have her come over to pick you up," she told Karen, after the meal was over.

"Okay," said Karen right away. Kristy saw that she was relieved to be going home. Normally she would have put up a big fight about it, but after sitting next to a cat at the dinner table for the last half an hour, Karen was in no mood to argue.

Karen changed out of her Lovely Lady clothes, and she was waiting at the door by the time her mother showed up. " 'Bye, Melody," said Karen.

"Meow," said Melody.

Kristy rolled her eyes and Mrs. Engle smiled. "That's a lovely cat you have there, ma'am," she said as she turned to walk off with Karen.

"Meow," said Melody.

And "meow" was all Melody said for the rest of the night. Kristy tried everything to end the game, but Melody was determined.

"How about Chutes and Ladders?" asked Kristy.

"Meow," said Melody.

"How about if we make some cookies?" asked Kristy.

"Meow," answered Melody.

"How about if we watch TV for a while?"

Kristy asked desperately. We try not to spend too much baby-sitting time watching TV with our charges, since we'd rather do fun, active stuff with them.

"Meow," said Melody.

Finally, Kristy gave up and let Melody do what she wanted to do, which was lie around purring and meowing, and letting Skylar and Bill treat her like a cat.

But just before bedtime, Kristy finally had her revenge. "Meow, meow," said Melody. "I'm hungry!"

"I've got the perfect snack for a hungry cat," said Kristy. She went to the kitchen, took two leftover fishsticks from the refrigerator, and placed them in a bowl. She brought it to Melody. "Here you go, kitty!" she said.

Melody looked up at her. There was no more purring, no more meowing. "Don't we have any cookies?" she asked, like the little girl she really was.

Kristy gave her a big hug — and then she gave her a couple of cookies, too.

CHAPTER 10

"Oh, no, another collection!" wailed Vanessa. She pointed into the little drawer in the end table. She and I had been assigned to clean up the living room, and the job was turning out to be a strange one. We kept discovering these odd little collections that Uncle Joe had made.

I'd found a bunch of pop-tops behind the geranium on the windowsill. Then Vanessa had found a tangle of thread tucked under the cushion of "his" chair. A pile of scrap paper was stuck beneath a magazine on the coffee table. And, in the drawer Vanessa had just opened, we found a stockpile of little tin-foil balls.

"I think this is how he spends all his time when we're away at school," she said, holding one up. "He must go all through the house every day, looking for stuff to add to his collections."

I shook my head. The situation with Uncle Joe had not gotten much better. He was still acting stiff and formal around us. He hadn't bothered to learn our names. And he spent a lot of each day dozing in his chair.

I was really, really trying to be patient. I was trying to put myself in his shoes and understand how it must feel to be old and achy and tired all the time. And I was still trying to convince myself that this visit was a good thing for him and for the Pike family.

But it was getting harder and harder. And I wasn't the only one having a hard time. The whole family was. The younger kids were confused by Uncle Joe's behavior, and hurt by the way he refused to learn their names. Vanessa and I were tired of feeling responsible for keeping our brothers and sisters quiet and well-behaved. And Mom and Dad were obviously worried about Uncle Joe.

"I think he was upstairs again today while we were out," Mom said to Dad one night during dinner. Uncle Joe had, as usual, left the table as soon as he'd finished eating. The rest of us were still picking at our spice-free tuna casserole.

"I think he's just a little bored and restless when none of us are home," answered Dad. "But I worry about him climbing those stairs. What if he falls when he's home alone?"

Uncle Joe was supposed to stay on the first floor. There was really no reason for him to go upstairs, since everything he needed was downstairs. But lately he seemed to like to wander around.

"I think my supervisor's getting upset about all the time I've taken off recently," said Mom. "I'm worried about Uncle Joe, too, but there's no way I can stay home every day to look after him."

Mom works part-time, and it's true that she's taken a lot of days off lately. She thought it was important to spend as much time with Uncle Joe as possible. He seemed to need more and more attention as time went on. And Mom didn't seem to mind spending time with him. But what if she lost her job?

To be totally honest, there were times when I actually wished that Uncle Joe had never come.

Like the time I got home from the mall last Saturday afternoon. Mom was working at the desk in the living room. She's been bringing a lot of work home lately, just so she won't fall behind because of the days she had taken off.

"Hi, honey," she said.

"Hi, Mom," I answered. "Where is everybody?" The house seemed awfully quiet.

"Well, let's see," she said, putting down her

pencil. "Vanessa's upstairs. I think she's working on a poem. Claire and Margo are playing dress-up in the rec room. And the boys are out playing with friends."

"What about Uncle Joe?" I asked.

"I think he's napping in the den," she said. "But why don't you check on him?"

I went to the door of the den and knocked lightly. No answer. I pushed the door open a crack and peeked inside. No Uncle Joe. The bed was made up neatly and his carefully folded pajamas were on the pillow.

"He's not there!" I said to Mom.

She looked up at me, her eyes round. "Oh, dear. And all this time I thought he was in his room. Where do you suppose he's gotten to?" she asked. "We'd better search the house."

We looked *everywhere*. We checked the whole house, top to bottom. No Uncle Joe.

"Maybe he went out with Dad somewhere," I said hopefully.

"No, I saw your father leave. He was on his way to the hardware store, and he was definitely alone in the car. Uncle Joe must have gone out by himself."

I volunteered to look for him, so I hopped on my bike and set out to search the neighborhood, while Mom stayed at home with my sisters. I rode all over, but I didn't see Uncle Joe anywhere. Finally I returned home, feeling defeated. Then, just as I flew up our driveway, I saw our neighbor, Mrs. Murphy, come out of her house. She was leading someone by the hand.

Uncle Joe!

"Mallory!" she called. "I'm glad to see you. This is your Uncle Joe, right?"

I nodded. What was he doing over at the Murphys'?

"Well, I guess he decided to pay us a visit," she said. "I just got home from the super-market and found him napping on our couch." She smiled kindly.

I was so, so embarrassed. For myself *and* for Uncle Joe. "I guess he went out for a little walk and got confused about where he was staying," I said. "He's still not really used to our house." I had parked my bike in the drive-way while we were talking, and now I headed over to Mrs. Murphy and Uncle Joe. I took Uncle Joe by the arm, gently, and led him back to our house. "Thanks!" I called to Mrs. Mur-phy. She waved and gave me an understand-ing look.

Uncle Joe has done some other strange things, too. For example, my mom decided that Uncle Joe might feel more like part of the family if he was given some responsibility around mealtimes, just like the rest of us. We take turns setting the table and clearing it and washing dishes — stuff like that. Anyway, Mom asked Uncle Joe to help her by wiping the dishes as she washed them. She figured that drying dishes was about the simplest job she could give him. He was just supposed to stack each dish on the counter as he finished it.

Well, Uncle Joe didn't seem to mind his new job. In fact, I think he liked it. He would stand by the sink in his suit, humming tunelessly while he polished each dish carefully. But after a while, he started to do odd things with the dishes. He'd put some of them back into the "dirty dishes" pile, and whoever was doing the dishes would end up washing half of them twice. (We caught on to that one pretty quickly.) Other times dishes would turn up in the strangest places. Uncle Joe would wander around with them and arrange them carefully on the TV stand, or in the oven. Once Mom even found some coffee cups in the washing machine!

Pretty soon Mom took Uncle Joe off dish duty. ("Too bad *I* never thought of hiding the dishes," said Nicky enviously.)

Uncle Joe was also having trouble with his sense of time. One morning, just after we'd finished having breakfast, he changed back into his pajamas as if it were time for bed. Another time he asked Mom why supper was so late that night, but it was only two in the afternoon! And every now and then I'd wake up and hear him shuffling around downstairs in the middle of the night.

Uncle Joe didn't *always* act weird. A lot of the time he seemed fine; he sat in his chair, he read the paper, and he ate his meals with our family. But I could tell Dad was feeling worried about Uncle Joe, and once in a while I'd catch my parents in the midst of a whispered conversation, both of them looking very serious.

Dad was awfully nice to Uncle Joe. We all tried to make him feel welcome, but Dad was the only one who could ever involve Uncle Joe in a real conversation. Sometimes at dinner they'd start talking about people they'd known years ago and Uncle Joe would look almost happy. The funny thing was that he never had any trouble at all remembering the names of every friend they'd ever gone fishing with. He remembered details about things that had happened forty-five years earlier, the same way I remember what happened to me yesterday. Yet he still couldn't tell me apart from Vanessa, or remember where he'd left his glasses.

One night, Dad and Uncle Joe were talking about this trip they'd once taken to the circus.

"Do you remember how we snuck Spanky into the tent?" Dad asked.

"I do," said Uncle Joe. "And I also remember how the crowd laughed when your dog ran out to join the clown parade."

Dad grinned."That was when we were asked to leave. But it was worth it, wasn't it?"

Uncle Joe didn't answer for a second. I saw Dad flash a concerned look at him.

"Uncle Joe?" he asked, touching the old man's arm.

Uncle Joe turned to look at Dad. He smiled politely at him. "I'm awfully sorry, sir," he said, "but I'm afraid I just can't seem to remember your name." Then he picked up his fork and took another careful bite of shepherd's pie.

Dad looked as if he'd been punched in the stomach. I glanced around the table to see whether everybody had seen and heard what had just happened, but my brothers and sisters were involved in other conversations. And Mom was busy refereeing a squabble between Claire and Margo.

"Uncle Joe," Dad said cautiously. "It's me, John Pike. You're visiting here with me and my family. We were just talking about the trip you and I took to the circus when I was a little boy." Dad sounded very gentle. He was giving Uncle Joe all the information he needed in order to remember where he was and what was going on.

"Of course, John," said Uncle Joe, as if the horrible episode had never happened. He looked insulted. "I was merely . . . *preoccupied* for a moment."

I exchanged glances with Dad. *Preoccupied?* Try "on Mars"! I couldn't believe what I'd just witnessed, but I could see by the look on Dad's face that he'd like me to keep it to myself. I gave him a nod, and I didn't tell anyone in the family. But I did tell Claudia that night on the phone. I'd called her because she was my "old-person expert." I hoped she'd be able to tell me something reassuring.

"Wow," she said. "That sounds really wild. I wonder if he had some kind of a stroke or something. That's what made Mimi act weird just before she died — a stroke."

"But he seems fine," I said. "It's just his thinking is a little off. Oh, Claud, it's so *weird* around here lately. And kind of scary . . ."

"Maybe you should tell that to your mom or dad," said Claudia. "Let them know that you're scared, and maybe they can help you understand what's going on."

I thanked Claudia for her advice, but I hung up feeling just as frustrated and confused as before. I *couldn't* go to Mom and Dad with my fears. They were worried enough already, and both of them had their hands full dealing with Uncle Joe. They didn't need a wacked-out daughter to add to their problems.

That night, though, the situation came to a head. I was fast asleep when I was awakened suddenly by a loud shriek. I jumped out of bed, my heart racing. The clock by my bed said three-thirty. I heard voices in the hall, so I went to investigate. Mom and Dad were both out there, comforting a sobbing Margo, who had been on her way to the bathroom. The three of them were in their pajamas — which made sense, since it was the middle of the night. But standing nearby was Uncle Joe, and he was fully dressed in his blue suit and starched white shirt. He looked as if he were on his way to church. Which, as it turned out, is exactly where he thought he was headed.

Margo calmed down and was put back to bed. Dad helped Uncle Joe downstairs and got *him* to bed. The house was quiet again. But something had changed. I'd seen it in Dad's eyes when he took Uncle Joe's arm in the hall.

Sure enough, the next morning Dad called an emergency family conference. We assembled in the rec room. Uncle Joe wasn't there — he was still sleeping, I think. Anyway, the door to his room was closed.

"I'm afraid we're going to have to cut Uncle Joe's visit short," said Dad. "He needs more care than we can give him here at home, and your mother and I have decided that he'll be better off back at Stoneybrook Manor."

I can't say I was dismayed by the news, except for two things. One, I had had such high hopes for this visit. And two, Dad looked so sad.

"Tell them the rest," said Mom gently. "They deserve to know what's been going on."

"Well," said Dad reluctantly, "when we picked up Uncle Joe at Stoneybrook Manor, the nurses told us they suspected he might be in the beginning stages of Alzheimer's disease. They asked us to watch for symptoms, and to bring him back for observation and tests if we felt it was necessary."

The younger kids weren't following this too well. "What's all-shiner's disease?" asked Claire.

"*Alzheimer's*," said Dad. "It's a disease that some people get when they are older. It can make them forget things, and act restless and confused. It affects their brain." He looked upset.

"That's why Uncle Joe's been acting weird?" asked Vanessa.

Dad nodded. "It probably explains most of his behavior," he said. "For example, the reason he's never learned your names is because people with Alzheimer's disease have a very hard time with short-term memory. They can remember things that happened years ago, but not things that happened this week." He gave a big sigh. "I think he'll be better off in a more stable, quiet environment."

"*We* can be more quiet!" said Nicky. I could see that he was worried by how sad Dad seemed, and he wanted to try to make things better.

Dad smiled. "I know," he said. "And I know that you've been trying really hard to make this visit work out. But what's happening is nobody's fault. And we have to do what's best for Uncle Joe."

Margo asked one last question. "Will Uncle Joe ever get better?"

Dad shook his head, looking sadder than ever. "Probably not, honey," he said. "But we'll do everything we can to make sure he's comfortable and well-taken care of."

CHAPTER 11

Thursday

Who ya gonna call? I love being
the official ghostbuster of Stoneybrook. Maybe I should advertise:
Is your house haunted? Are you
pestered by poltergeists? Bothered
by boogeymen? Are there phantoms
in your phlower garden? Spirits in
your spare room? Don't delay —
call Dawn today! Seriously, Mal, you
had perfect timing. I was just
brushing up on my ghostbusting
techniques by reading this neat
book called *How to Find a Ghost.* So
when you called, I was ready for action.

I had been thinking for days about what had happened the last time I was at the Craines'. In fact, I couldn't *stop* thinking about those letters we'd found. Kennedy Graham had been such an odd, reclusive man, but he'd come to love that cat so much. So much that, even after it died, he heard it meowing! The lonely man, the white cat, the meowing from the attic — it gave me the creeps, to tell you the truth. And I started to wonder (now please, don't think I'm totally nuts) if maybe Ghost Cat really was a ghost.

Could it be? Could Ghost Cat and Tinker be one and the same? I'll tell you, I had a few strange dreams, just from thinking about the possibility. But you know what? I was kind of glad for the distraction, glad for something *besides* Uncle Joe to think about.

Anyway, one night I had a brainstorm. If I was having a ghost problem, or at least a *possible* ghost problem, the person to talk to was Dawn. She is fascinated by ghosts. In fact, she's sure that there may be one living in this secret passage in her house. (Dawn's house is really old. I wouldn't be surprised if there were *several* ghosts living in it!) Dawn reads everything she can about ghosts, and she knows an incredible amount about different types of ghosts and what they do.

When I called Dawn, she immediately grew excited by my idea. "What we have to do," she said, "is run some tests on Ghost Cat. Tests that will prove whether he really is a flesh-and-blood cat, or if he's *something else*."

Her voice sounded *so* creepy when she said "something else." "Um — do you know how to *do* tests like that?" I asked. The idea made me a little nervous.

"Sure!" she said. "No problem. When do you want me to see the cat?"

I gulped. "Well," I said. "I'm supposed to sit at the Craines' on Thursday afternoon, and I guess — "

"Great!" she said. "I'll be there."

So that's how Dawn came to be with me at the Craines' house that Thursday afternoon. I had called Mrs. Craine the night before to make sure it was okay if a friend visited with me (I didn't mention the G-word at all), and she had said it was fine with her.

The girls were excited about having two sitters that day. And they liked Dawn right away. "Hi, Dawn!" said Sophie. "Want to come see my room?"

"No, *my* room!" yelled Margaret.

"Play with Barbie B.?" asked Katie shyly, holding out her favorite doll.

"You should be honored," I whispered to

Dawn. "Not too many people get to play with Barbie B."

"Barbie B. looks just like any *regular* Barbie to me," Dawn whispered back.

I nodded. "She is. But she's pretty special to Katie." Then I raised my voice. "Margaret! Sophie! Come over here. We have something to tell you. We're going to play a really fun game today," I continued as they huddled close to me and Dawn.

"What?" asked Sophie.

"We're going ghost-hunting!" I announced.

"Yea!" yelled Margaret.

"Oh, boy!" shouted Sophie.

Katie beamed. They loved the idea. I'm pretty sure they are too young to be truly afraid of ghosts. Plus, they've all seen the Ghostbusters cartoon, so they know that hunting ghosts can be fun and exciting.

"Dawn is our ghostbuster," I said. "She's going to make sure that if there are any ghosts in this house, they're taken care of." I didn't want to bring up the idea that Ghost Cat was under suspicion — at least, not yet.

"What do we do first?" asked Sophie.

"Let's show her the attic," suggested Margaret.

"Great," said Dawn. "Ghosts love attics."

We headed upstairs, flashlights in hand.

The girls began to give Dawn a tour of the attic.

"There's the table Ghost Cat was hiding under when we first saw him," said Margaret.

"And there's the hat box where we found the letters," said Sophie.

"Right, the letters," said Dawn. "I'd like to see those." She was holding something in her hand and peering at it as she shone the beam of her flashlight over it.

"What's that?" I asked.

"A thermometer," she said. "I just wanted to check on the temperature up here. A lot of times there will be a distinct chill in the air when ghosts are present."

"Oh," I said, impressed. Dawn seemed so — so *professional*.

After a little while, Dawn said she'd seen enough, so we trooped back downstairs. Margaret ran to find the letters, while Dawn took a break from ghostbusting to play a quick game of patty-cake with Katie.

"Here they are!" said Margaret, waving the letters in the air as she came back into the room. "And here's a picture of that weird Kennedy Graham."

"He wasn't so weird," I said, feeling defensive. I guess I was thinking of Uncle Joe. "He was just old — and lonely."

"Let's see the letters," said Dawn. She read

through them quickly. "Hmmm . . ." she said. "I wonder . . ."

"What? What?" asked Margaret and Sophie.

"I wonder if Ghost Cat really *is* a ghost cat!" Dawn said.

I'd known it was coming, but the girls were taken by surprise. Their eyes lit up.

"A real ghost?" asked Sophie.

"How do we find out if that's true?" asked Margaret.

Some kids might have been scared, but not these two. Even Katie was excited, although she was too young to know what was going on. She banged a spoon against her high chair. "Dost!" she cried.

Dawn was in her element. "Well," she said, "there are some tests we can do. First, we'll check the temperature in that laundry room — "

"Hey, I just thought of something," interrupted Margaret. "How can that cat be a ghost? He's a *cat*! Aren't ghosts always people?"

"Nope," said Dawn. "In fact, this book I just read said that up to twenty percent of all ghosts are animals, or even objects. And the most common animal ghosts are dogs and cats!"

"Wow!" said Margaret, in a hushed voice.

"Anyway," said Dawn, "as I was saying,

first we'll check the temperature in there. Cooler temperatures can indicate ghosts. Then we can test for the presence of ectoplasm with this meter." She reached into the knapsack she'd brought with her and pulled out a weird little box covered with dials and knobs.

"Where did you get that?" I asked.

"I sent away for it," she said. She admired it for a moment. "It was advertised in the back of a *Ghostly Tales* comic book."

I nodded, though I wasn't sure that what she was holding was much of a scientific tool. It looked as if it was made out of cardboard. Heavy-duty cardboard, but still cardboard.

"Well, let's get started!" I said. Dawn could probably talk about ectoplasm levels all day, but personally, I was ready for action.

We opened the door of the laundry room cautiously, expecting Ghost Cat to dash out. But by that time, he had started to feel comfortable in there. He was curled up on top of the dryer, and he glanced at us with mild curiosity when we came in.

Dawn looked closely at Ghost Cat. "Hmmm . . ." she said, making a few notes in the little book she was carrying. "He doesn't seem to be transparent at all."

"What does transparent mean?" asked Sophie.

"It means like plastic wrap," explained Margaret. "Like when you can see through something."

"Ghost Cat isn't like plastic wrap!" said Sophie indignantly.

"Right," said Dawn. "But some ghosts are. It's just one of the things to check for when you're looking for ghosts." She was taking the temperature in the room and marking it down in her book. Then she held up her ectoplasm meter, pointing it toward Ghost cat. She adjusted a few knobs, checked and re-checked the dials, and adjusted the knobs again. She frowned as she looked at the main dial. "No reading," she said. She banged her hand against the side of the box, then checked the dial again. "Hmph," she said, putting the box down. "I can't tell whether it's working or not." She seemed disappointed. "Oh well, what can you expect for five ninety-nine?" She gave the box a little kick.

"What's next?" asked Margaret.

"Well," said Dawn, "The next thing I think we need is to take a picture." She pulled a Polaroid camera out of her knapsack.

Margaret pulled Sophie and Katie in front of the sink. "Say cheese," she instructed her sisters. She gave Dawn a big smile. What a ham!

"A picture of the *cat*, you silly!" said Dawn.

"Oh," said Margaret, clearly disappointed.

I gave Dawn a Look.

"Well, I guess we can take a picture of you guys, too," said Dawn. She pointed the camera at the girls and the flash went off. Then she took a picture of the cat. He still didn't move, just sat there blinking after the flash.

We waited for the pictures to develop, and then Dawn put them side by side. "Look!" she said. "The picture of the cat is lighter and less focused!" she sounded really excited. "This could be important!"

I hated to bring her down, but I had to point something out. "I think it's just because the one of the girls has had more time to develop," I said. And sure enough, by the time I'd gotten the words out, the picture of the cat had become strong and clear.

"Well," said Dawn. "This isn't looking good. I mean — " She corrected herself. "I mean if you happened to be hoping for a ghost," she said. "I'm sure you girls would be happier if he was just a regular cat, right?"

Margaret nodded.

"I have one more test," said Dawn. "Actually it's two tests in one. But this will prove once and for all whether or not this cat is a ghost." She shooed the rest of us out of the laundry room, but left the door open so we could see what she was doing. Then she took a little plastic bag out of her knapsack and sprinkled some white powder on the floor. "Flour," she explained, before we could ask. "If he's a ghost, his footprints won't show." Then she reached back into her knapsack and came up with some thumbtacks and thread. She strung the thread across the lower part of the door, holding it in place with the thumbtacks. "A ghost would go through the string without breaking it," she said.

She stepped carefully out of the laundry room. "Now all we have to do is get him to come out of there," she said.

"I know how to make him come!" cried Margaret. She ran for his box of kitty treats. Then she shook it outside the door, and the cat came running. He ran right through the flour, leaving big, clear footprints. Then he broke through the string. Margaret gave him a treat. "Good kitty," she said, patting him.

"I'm *glad* he's not a ghost," said Sophie. She and Katie bent to pat his head.

Dawn and I looked at each other. I could see that Dawn was disappointed. Then I saw her frown. "What's that noise?" she asked. I stood still and listened. A meowing sound. Coming from upstairs. Dawn raised her eyebrows. A shiver ran down my spine. And then the phone rang.

"Hello?" I asked, grabbing the phone. My heart was beating fast.

"Hello, I'm calling about your ad in the paper — the ad about the white cat. I'm sure he's mine. Has he got a small nick in his right ear?" The man's voice was brusque. He almost sounded rude.

"Yes!" I said. I'd noticed that nick when I was looking at the picture Dawn had taken.

"His name is Rasputin," the man said.

"Well, you can come and get him tonight," I said. (Mrs. Craine had told me not to let anyone who might answer the ad come by while I was baby-sitting. She wanted to be home when a stranger arrived.)

"I can't," said the man shortly. "I'm out of town. But I'll be there in two days' time." He hung up without saying good-bye.

Well, that was weird. If this guy was out of town, how did he see the paper? And couldn't he get here sooner, if he really missed his cat? But I didn't have time to worry about my questions. We needed to clean up the flour before Mrs. Craine got home!

CHAPTER 12

I was beginning to feel as if I was living two lives. When I was at the Craines', all I could think about was Ghost Cat, and Kennedy Graham, and mysterious meowing sounds, and strange phone calls. When I was at home, all I could think about was Uncle Joe. I'd gone to the library to try to find out a little more about Alzheimer's disease, and what I found out made me feel sad.

The disease is kind of a mystery, so far. Nobody knows exactly what the cause of it is, and nobody knows how to treat it, either. It's a *degenerative* disease, which means that it usually just keeps getting worse and worse. I felt so bad for Uncle Joe. I hoped he wasn't too aware of what was happening to him. I knew he'd had a long, full life, and I knew the people at Stoneybrook Manor would take good care of him. Still, it was really sad.

Saturday was going to be Uncle Joe's last

day at our house. Mom and Dad were going to be out all morning. The people at Stoneybrook Manor had asked them to come in for a conference before they brought Uncle Joe back. The doctors and nurses wanted to know everything Mom and Dad could tell them about his condition and his state of mind.

Jessi had come over to help me baby-sit that morning. I was glad. She'd never met Uncle Joe and this would be her last chance. Also, I hadn't been able to spend much time with her lately, and I'd missed her.

"I loved *A Wrinkle in Time,*" she said, as soon as she walked in the door. "I just finished it this morning."

I'd told her about that book as soon as I'd finished it, because I knew she'd like it as much as I did. It's great having a best friend who loves to read. We're always recommending books to each other, and we have so much fun talking about them. There's something special about reading a great book and then discussing it with someone you like; it makes you appreciate the book — *and* your friend — in new and interesting ways.

"Wasn't it great when Meg was with Aunt Beast?" I asked. "That was one of my favorite parts."

"Mine, too," said Jessi. "And then when

she figured out how powerful her love for her family could really be."

Just then Uncle Joe wandered into the hall where we were still standing. He gave Jessi a quizzical look. She glanced at me, suddenly nervous, but then she got hold of herself.

"Hello, Mr. Pike," said Jessi. "My name is Jessi Ramsey. I'm glad to meet you." She smiled, but didn't stick out her hand to shake his. I'd told her about Claud's experience and she'd obviously remembered it.

Uncle Joe nodded to her. He didn't smile, but he wasn't frowning, either. "I believe I'll go to my room now," he said to me. "I'll pack my belongings and I may also take a short nap." He still sounded as formal and polite as the day he had arrived. And, apparently, he still hadn't learned my name. Now I at least knew *why*.

"Okay, Uncle Joe," I said. "Let me know if I can help you with anything."

He nodded again. "You're very kind," he said. Then he turned and left.

I watched him walk away. Then I raised my eyebrows at Jessi. "Very kind?" I said. "That's the first time he said anything like *that*."

"He doesn't seem so bad," Jessi replied. "I mean, he didn't say anything nasty, and he didn't seem confused or anything."

"He has his good days and his bad days," I said. "But he's never really *nasty*, exactly. Just . . . just not very tactful, I guess."

"My grandmother was kind of like that," said Jessi. "I used to think *she* thought that because she was old she didn't have to be polite anymore. She'd say the most hurtful things, like 'My, haven't *you* gotten fat,' to my mother, or 'Losing your hair pretty quickly, aren't you?' to my father. It used to make me so mad. I felt like saying mean things back to her, about her wrinkles and stuff. But then, after I'd spent some more time around her, I figured out that she only said those things because she wasn't comfortable making small talk. She didn't know what to say, so she'd just say the first thing that came into her mind. She didn't *mean* to be nasty or rude."

I thought for a minute. "It's pretty easy to make snap judgments about people's personalities, isn't it?" I said. My family had been so ready for the Uncle Joe Dad had described that the *real* Uncle Joe had been a shock. But maybe we still didn't know who Uncle Joe *truly* was. Finding that out would take time, and that was something we didn't have. I realized that we'd probably never get to know him now.

Boy, I was really having some heavy thoughts! But it's hard to get too philosophical in the Pike household. Someone usually interrupts you.

"Hi, Jessi!" shouted Nicky as he ran into the hall. "Guess what?"

Jessi smiled at him. "What?" she asked.

"We're almost ready for the Pike Olympics!" he said. He grabbed her hand and started to pull her along. "Come see!"

She looked back at me and gave a helpless shrug. I followed as Nicky led us into the rec room. "Oh, my lord!" I said, when I saw what my brothers and sisters had done to the place. There were upturned chairs in the middle of the room. The rug had been rolled up and Margo was walking along it as if it were a balance beam. The couch pillows were strewn all over the floor, and some were in towering piles.

Byron grinned at Jessi and me. "Neat, huh?" he said.

"Neat" was not exactly the word that came to *my* mind.

"We're going to have an obstable course!" shouted Claire.

"*Obstacle*," corrected Jordan. "*Obstacle* course. And it's not for you, Claire. That event's only for older kids."

Claire pouted.

"But you get to do the hopping race!" said

Vanessa, trying to cheer Claire up. "And you're a really, really good hopper. I bet you'll win."

Claire looked a little happier.

"Why are those pillows all piled up?" asked Jessi.

"That's for the leapfrogging event," explained Adam.

Jessi nodded. "I see," she said. She looked around the room. "Maybe we ought to move this lamp out of the way," she said, picking up a ceramic lamp.

"Good idea," I replied. I scouted the room for other breakable items, and ended up putting a mirror and two framed pictures into the closet along with the lamp. I turned the TV to the wall. You might think I was being a little overcareful, but you never know with my brothers and sisters.

"Let the games begin!" I said, as soon as the room seemed Pike-proof.

What a scene. This was no orderly Olympics. At least three events were going on at any given moment, and at least four kids were yelling, "Mallory, Jessi! Look at me!" My head was spinning. I watched Jordan leapfrog neatly over a huge pile of sofa cushions. Nicky followed behind him, but Nicky's leap wasn't quite so neat. He sprawled on the floor, surrounded by the pillows.

"Are you okay?" I asked.

"I'm *great*," he answered. "That was totally cool. I want to do it again." He piled up the cushions again and took another running leap.

Claire and Margo were hopping around the room. They were supposed to be hopping on one foot, but neither of them was all that great at it. They kept switching feet, and occasionally hopping on both feet. Vanessa was the judge for that event. "Good, Claire," she called. "Nice hopping. Okay, Margo, one more time over the course and you're done. Whoops! That's all right. We can pick up those magazines later."

The room was full of noise and activity, and I was totally caught up in it. Suddenly I felt Jessi's elbow in my ribs. "What?" I asked. I looked around frantically. Then I saw him.

Uncle Joe was standing in the doorway.

"Uncle Joe!" I said. "Did we disturb you? I'm sorry. I — "

But Uncle Joe just held up a hand and shook his head slightly. He was watching Adam go through the obstacle course. And I saw — or at least, I *thought* I saw — a tiny smile on his lips. But before I could get a better look, he'd turned and left the room.

"We better cool it," I said to Jessi. "I mean, he didn't yell at us or anything, but — "

"Yeah, you're right," she said. "This *is* a

pretty noisy activity. And it's his last day. We should make it a nice quiet one for him."

"Okay, kids," I shouted. "Olympics are over for today."

Big groans.

"You can do it again tomorrow, but right now we're going to do something a little quieter," I said, thinking quickly. "We're going to — we're going to have a coloring contest!"

"Yea!" shouted Margo. She loves to color.

Vanessa looked at me skeptically. "A coloring contest?" she asked.

"Right," I said. "Everybody has to draw a picture of our family, and we'll give the winning picture to Uncle Joe. He can put it in his room at Stoneybrook Manor."

I don't know where I got that idea, but it worked. The room quieted down right away as everybody rummaged around for paper and crayons and markers. Once the kids were busy drawing, Jessi and I put the couch back together and sat down to talk. I filled her in on the latest news about Ghost Cat, and she told me about the production her ballet school was rehearsing for. It was great to catch up.

"All done!" said Claire, bringing her picture over to me. "That's Mommy," she said, pointing at a figure with wild, curly hair, "and Daddy, and you, and Vanessa — "

"Beautiful picture," I said, before she had a

chance to run down the whole list of names. She beamed. Then, one after another, Vanessa, Margo, Jordan, Adam, and Byron brought us their pictures. They were all terrific.

"Where's Nicky?" I asked, suddenly realizing he was gone.

"I don't know," said Adam, "but here's his picture." He picked up a drawing that had been left on the floor. "Look," he said. "This one has Uncle Joe *in* it."

Sure enough, Nicky's picture included a blue-suited, spectacles-wearing figure. "That's great," I said. I made up my mind right away to tell Nicky he'd won the contest. But where was he? "I wonder where he went?" I said out loud. "Let's look," I added to Jessi. "You guys can stay here and draw some more if you want." Jessi and I walked down the hall and checked the kitchen and the dining room. No Nicky. Then I heard giggles from the living room. I gestured to Jessi, and she followed me to the doorway. We peeked inside.

There was Nicky — sitting on Uncle Joe's lap! Uncle Joe was holding a white handkerchief that was folded to look like a mouse. "Nice little mousie," he said, stroking it. Then he made it *run* up his arm, just like a real mouse. Nicky laughed.

"Do it again, Uncle Joe!" he said.

Jessi and I looked at each other wide-eyed. I couldn't believe what I was seeing. Then Uncle Joe glanced up and saw us. "Young Nick here reminded me about this old trick," he said. "I'd forgotten all about it."

Nick! He'd actually remembered somebody's name!

I was speechless.

"I see that you're shocked to see me doing this," said Uncle Joe. "I know I've been rather quiet for the past weeks, and I'm sorry. It's just that I'm quite set in my ways, and it's difficult for me to be around so many people."

"That — that's okay," I said. "I understand."

"I'm sorry that I must be leaving you just as I'm beginning to become accustomed to your family's ways," he said.

I was amazed. Claudia had been right! It was just a matter of the Pikes getting used to Uncle Joe, and of him getting used to us.

The rest of the day flew by. I can't say that Uncle Joe turned into some jolly Santa-like person, but he did show us another side of him. He pulled a nickel out of Margo's ear. He did string tricks for the triplets. He let Claire try on his glasses. He even read several of Vanessa's poems. He was much more comfortable dealing with us one or two at a time.

We were sad to see him leave that afternoon,

but as Mom and Dad explained to us, Stoney-brook Manor really was the right place for him. "One good day doesn't mean the disease is gone," said Dad. "He'll need plenty of care in the days to come."

"I'm so glad he *did* have this good day," said Mom. "The doctor told us that Alzheimer's doesn't usually change people's personalities, and now I can see that he was right." She looked at Dad. "The Uncle Joe you remember still exists, but he's much older now and he takes longer to feel comfortable with new people."

I smiled, remembering my first glimpse of Uncle Joe with Nicky on his lap. They certainly *had* looked comfortable together. "I'm just glad he finally did," I said.

CHAPTER 13

"M ine!"

"No, *mine!*"

Katie and Sophie were standing in the living room, their faces pushed together. They were each holding one arm of a teddy bear I'd never seen before, they were yelling at the top of their lungs.

"Girls," I said helplessly. "How about taking turns?" I had no idea which one of them might be the real owner.

"It's mine," confided Margaret, coming up behind me. "I mean, it was mine when I was a baby. I just found it at the bottom of my toy box. They think it's a new toy, and they both want it."

"Mine!" said Sophie.

"*Mine!*" shrieked Katie.

I sighed. "I think it's time to put Teddy away for a while," I said, as I gently pried it loose from their fingers. Sometimes that's the only solution in cases like these. At least, it's Step One of the solution.

Sophie's jaw dropped. "Hey — " she said.

Katie's eyes grew round. She opened her mouth wide, as if she were getting ready to scream. It was time for Step Two of the solution I was using. Guess what Step Two is. Right. *Distraction*.

"Hey, let's go visit Ghost Cat, okay?" I said. I started off in the direction of the laundry room, hoping the girls would follow me. I turned to check. Katie was still standing there, trying to decide whether or not to have a tantrum.

"It's his last day here, you know," I added. Katie closed her mouth and started to trot after me.

"Dost tat!" she said.

"His name's *Rasputin*," said Margaret. "That's what the man said, right?" she asked me.

"Right," I said. "Funny name for a cat, isn't it?"

"I guess. But we really couldn't have called him Ghost Cat anymore anyway. Dawn proved that he *isn't* a ghost."

"That's true," I said. And it *was* true. Dawn's tests had been pretty foolproof. But something funny was still going on at the Craines', something that made me feel that the Ghost Cat mystery wasn't over quite yet.

"Hi, Rasputin," said Margaret, opening the laundry room door. "Hi, kitty!"

The white cat jumped down from the dryer and rubbed himself against Margaret's legs.

"Wow," I said. "He's gotten friendlier, hasn't he?"

"He started doing that as soon as I called him by his right name," said Margaret. "Isn't that funny?"

"Hi, tat," said Katie, bending to pat him.

"Mine!" said Sophie. She seemed to be in a *very* possessive mood that day.

"No, Sophie," I said. "He's not yours, or Katie's, or Margaret's. He belongs to someone else, and he's coming to get him today."

Sophie looked like she was about to cry. "I want Rasputin to *stay*," she said.

"I know," I replied. "But his owner loves him and he wants him back." I wished I could tell Sophie what I had found out the day before when Mrs. Craine called during our meeting. She told me that Mr. Craine would be coming home in time to be there when the man showed up at five-thirty to pick up his cat. But she'd also told me that, since the girls seemed to love the cat so much, she and Mr. Craine were thinking about getting them their very own cat.

If only I could have told Sophie! I knew the

news would cheer her up. But Mrs. Craine had asked me *not* to tell, not until she and Mr. Craine were sure about their decision.

"That was fun, doing those ghost tests with Dawn," said Margaret, as she patted the cat.

"I know," I said. "Hey! Let's do some other tests on the cat, okay?" I wanted to make the girls forget that the cat would be gone by the end of the day. "Let's see," I said. "How about a cat I.Q. test?"

"What's an I.Q. test?" asked Sophie. I'd caught her interest.

"It measures how smart you are," I said. "Usually it's for people, but we can make up one for a cat. What kinds of things do smart cats do?"

"Catch mice!" shouted Margaret.

"Come when you call them," said Sophie.

"Tat!" yelled Katie.

"Okay," I said. "So let's make a test. Where's that toy mouse your father brought home for the cat?"

Margaret ran to find it. "Here it is!" she said.

"All right, now, we'll put the mouse behind this closet door," I went on, "and time how long it takes the cat to find it. We'll give him three chances."

I hid the mouse, making sure the cat saw me do it, and then checked my watch. It only took him twenty seconds to "catch" the mouse! I hid it two more times. He had no trouble finding it.

"He's *fast*!" said Sophie. "That means he has a lot of I.Q., right?"

I laughed. "Right. But let's try the next test. We'll go outside the door and call him by different names, to find out which one he answers to."

Leaving the door open, I herded the girls outside the room. Then I started to call out all kinds of made-up names. "Um . . . Snowflake!" I called. "Chalky!" I was trying to think of names for white cats. "Pearl!"

I peeked around the door to look at the cat. The girls looked over my shoulder. He was just sitting there, washing his face with his paw.

"Let me try!" said Margaret. "Milky!" she cried. The cat didn't move.

Sophie pushed her way to the front of our little crowd. "Ghost Cat?" she called cautiously. I wondered if he'd respond to *that*, but he didn't.

Then it was Katie's turn. "Jennifer!" she said, decisively.

We all cracked up. What a name for a cat! Especially a male cat. Of course, the cat didn't answer to that one, either. It was time for the final test.

I said the name quietly. "Rasputin?"

He was out of that room like a shot, and he rubbed himself around my ankles, purring, until I bent to pick him up. "Boy, I guess you do know your name, don't you?" I asked him. "You're a pretty smart cat."

"He'd *have* to be smart," said Margaret, "to find his way into our attic the way he did."

I agreed. "I wonder why he ran away from his owner in the first place?" I mused. "And why he came to *your* house?"

"Yeah," said Margaret. "And why didn't his owner come to get him right away?"

"Maybe the man doesn't really want him," said Sophie. "Then we can keep him."

Uh-oh. "No, he definitely wants him back," I said. "Your mom told me that he has called two more times. He didn't say any more about who he was or where he lived, but he said he was coming to get the cat. Today."

Sophie stuck her lower lip out.

"How about if we give the cat one last meal while he's living here?" I asked quickly. "We'll give him something special, so he'll remember us." I led the way into the kitchen.

Margaret burrowed into one of the cabinets and came up with a jar of olives. "These are a special kind," she said. "My dad loves them."

I shook my head. "I don't think the cat would appreciate them," I said.

Sophie pulled out a box of Alpha bits cereal. "My favorite," she said. "Let's give him a bowlful."

"Well, he might like the *milk* we put on them, but I don't really think he'd eat those little ABC's," I said. "You should save them for yourself."

I pulled the milk out of the fridge and poured some in a small bowl. I also found a half-empty can of tuna, and somehow didn't think Mrs. Craine would mind if I gave it to the cat. I put the food down on the floor in the spot where he always ate, and called the cat. "Rasputin!" I called. "Come, kittykitty-kitty!"

Rasputin trotted in, heading straight for the tuna. As soon as he'd finished it, he turned to the milk and lapped that up.

"He really loves it," said Margaret. "I wonder what his owner usually feeds him."

"Well, probably nothing this special all the time," I said. "But I hope he gets a treat once in a while."

"I would give him milk every single day if he lived with us," said Sophie wistfully. She gazed at the cat. "Look! It's on his whiskers, and he's licking it off."

Rasputin finished off the milk, shook himself, and sat down to wash his face. The girls watched his every move. The kitchen was silent — and then I heard it. A meowing noise! It was coming from upstairs. I almost jumped out of my seat, but the girls didn't seem to notice the sound. I held my breath and listened. Maybe I'd been thinking about this Ghost Cat business too much.

Then I heard the noise again. This time I got up and walked toward the stairs, trying to pin down exactly where the noise was coming from. The girls, engrossed in watching Rasputin wash himself, ignored me completely. I listened again. The sound was coming from the attic.

I went back to the kitchen and sat down to think. How could I hear meowing from the attic when Rasputin was sitting right in front of me? It didn't seem likely that *another* cat had found its way up there, and anyway, we'd looked around up there so many times we would have seen it if it had. I thought about lonely old Kennedy Graham. I thought about his little white cat named Tinker. The cat that died and left him all alone. Could the ghost of Tinker be here, looking for its master?

I was really getting spooked.

Luckily, Mr. Craine came home before the girls noticed anything. "Hi, Mallory," he said, tossing his coat onto a chair. "I hope I'm on time."

"Daddy!" yelled all three girls at once. They

scrambled to be the first on his lap.

"You're right on time," I said. "Rasputin's owner is due any minute." I glanced at the clock over the stove. It said five twenty-five.

"Guess what? We tested Rasputin's Q.I.!" said Sophie. "And he has a lot of it, too."

Mr. Craine looked confused.

"She means I.Q.," explained Margaret. "We gave him a cat I.Q. test, and he did really well."

"He did, did he?" asked Mr. Craine, raising his eyebrows at me and trying to hide his smile. "I always knew he was an especially smart cat."

"Muk!" cried Katie.

"Milk?" asked Mr. Craine. "You want some milk?" He started to get up.

"No," said Katie. "Tat!"

"She's trying to tell you we gave the cat some milk," I explained. "For his last meal. I hope that was okay."

"Oh, sure," said Mr. Craine. "We want him to remember us, don't we?"

"That's what Mallory said," said Margaret.

Just then, the doorbell rang. "That must be him," I said. "Rasputin's owner."

Mr. Craine answered the door, and the girls and I followed him. I guess I should have left as soon as Mr. Craine came home, but I was dying to see what this mystery man looked like.

Mr. Craine opened the door. I took one look at the man standing there and felt like I was going to pass out. "Oh, my lord!" I said, under my breath.

Margaret tugged at my hand. "He looks just like the man in the picture," she whispered to me.

She was right. This man was the spitting image of Kennedy Graham! Same white hair and rugged face. He even had a little scar under his eye, in exactly the same place as the man in the picture!

I'm sure my mouth was hanging open. I must have looked like an idiot. But Mr. Craine didn't seem to notice. He'd invited the man in, and the man had refused his offer, so now Mr. Craine asked me to get the cat.

I ran to find Rasputin, and when I did, I carried him gently to the front door and put him into the man's arms. "Thank you," said the stranger. He handed me something. "And thank you, little girls, for taking such good care of my cat," he added, handing something to each girl. Then he put Rasputin into the carrying case he'd brought, said good-bye, and left.

I looked down at my hand and saw a five-dollar bill. Margaret held up another one, and Sophie and Katie examined theirs. "Wow!" I said, getting my breath back. "He sure was generous!"

"He was," said Mr. Craine. "And that reminds me, I've still got to pay you." He headed back to the kitchen to find his wallet.

The girls and I looked at each other. "Who *was* that?" asked Sophie.

"I think he was a ghost!" said Margaret. "I think the cat *and* the man are both ghosts."

You know what? I couldn't argue with her. But I didn't want to scare her, either. "Well," I said, "the main thing is that Rasputin seemed happy to see him. I think they belong together. The Ghost Cat mystery is over."

I *sounded* sure of myself. But I wasn't. Not at all.

CHAPTER 14

It was a Sunday morning, and the Pike household was in an uproar. I know, I know. What else is new? The Pike household is *always* in an uproar. Or at least it seems that way.

But there's nothing like a family trip to make us completely crazy. By family trip, I mean all ten of us going to the same place and leaving at the same time. That doesn't happen too often, and I think I know why. If we tried to do it on any regular basis, Mom and Dad would have more than a few gray hairs each by now.

Where were we going? To visit Uncle Joe. We wanted to see how he was doing at Stoneybrook Manor. You know, a few weeks ago I wouldn't have wanted to go on this outing. Or if I'd gone, it would have been because I felt guilty, or obligated. Visiting Uncle Joe would *not* have sounded like a fun thing to do. But thanks to Nicky, I'd gotten a glimpse of what Uncle Joe *could* be like, and I thought he might be a pretty neat person once I got to know him. So anyway, I was looking forward to the visit.

Everybody else was, too. You'd think we were heading for the White House to meet the President. Everybody was in a panic over what to wear, how to wrap their presents, and what to bring to "show Uncle Joe."

"But I *have* to wear my Lucy dress!" wailed Claire. "I *have* to!" Claire has this favorite dress that we call the Lucy dress because it looks like something that Lucy in the Peanuts comic strip would wear. It has a flouncy skirt, and it's striped in blue and black. Claire has worn it practically every day for the past six months. She even sleeps in it sometimes.

"Honey," said Mom, "I'm sorry, but it's in the washing machine right now. You're going to have to find something else to wear."

Claire stamped her foot and pouted, but she saw that she wasn't going to get anywhere with Mom. "Okay, you silly-billy-goo-goo," she said. (Claire calls people that all the time. We're used to it.) "But I'm still going to wear my party shoes, no matter what!" Claire's supposed to save her party shoes for special occasions, otherwise she puts them on every day and they wear out fast. I guess Mom was willing to call this visit a special occasion since she didn't argue.

"I bet Uncle Joe will think *my* picture is the best," said Jordan, holding it up so I could see it.

"No way, José," said Adam. "Mine is *much* cooler." He held up his picture.

"You guys are both dreaming," said Byron. "My picture is totally cool and Uncle Joe will definitely like it best."

"They're all great," I said, "and I'm sure he'll like them all. But I don't think the people who run Stoneybrook Manor are going to let you guys in dressed like that. You'd better put some clothes on, okay?"

The three of them looked at each other. Byron was wearing one sock and a pair of Bart Simpson surfer shorts. Jordan was wearing a pair of Mets sweatpants — and that was all. Adam was still in his He-Man pajamas.

"I think we look great!" said Adam, grinning at me. "Better than *you*, you dweeb."

I silently counted to ten. We didn't need any squabbles that morning. "At least I'm a fully *dressed* dweeb," I said, giving Adam a noogie on the top of his head. "And it's time for my dweeby brothers to get dressed, too."

They just stood there, as if they were daring me to get mad at them. "Come on, you guys,"

I said. They didn't move. Then Vanessa drifted down the hall.

"Want to hear the poem I wrote for Uncle Joe?" she asked. "It's five pages long."

The triplets were out of there before I could blink an eye.

I smiled at Vanessa. She'd gotten them moving, even if it *was* an accident. "I'd love to hear it sometime," I said, "but not right now." I started to edge around her. "I'm sure it's a very nice poem," I said. As soon as I got past her, I rolled my eyes and heaved a sigh of relief. Vanessa's poems are sometimes a little hard to sit through.

She followed me down the hall. "Let me just read you the first part," she said. "It begins like this: O, Uncle Joe, we miss you so, we were so sad to see you go — "

"Nice, Vanessa," I called, as I hurried away.

Half an hour later, our family was finally piled into the car. Nicky was carrying the picture he'd drawn during our coloring contest. Adam had helped him make a frame for it out of old model airplane parts. Margo was carrying a pencil jar she'd made at school — an orange juice can covered with construction paper. I wasn't sure if Uncle Joe *needed* a pencil jar, but I figured he'd appreciate the thought that went into making the gift.

"All set?" asked Dad, as he backed down the driveway.

"No!" I cried. Dad screeched to a halt.

"What is it, Mallory?" he asked, sounding kind of impatient.

"I forgot the cookies I made," I said. "I'll just be a second, really." I jumped out of the car and ran back into the house. I couldn't believe it. I'd been so busy making sure my brothers and sisters were ready that I'd blanked out on my own plans. I grabbed the tin of cookies from the kitchen counter and ran back to the car. Finally, we were on our way.

The drive to Stoneybrook Manor isn't a long one, but it took *us* a while. Why? Well, one of the things you should know about Margo is that she has a very, very weak stomach. She gets carsick if she *thinks* about taking a trip. We had to pull over twice before we'd even left the neighborhood. Luckily, Margo had been too excited to eat very much that morning. But Dad's so used to her stomach that he doesn't hesitate to pull over the second he hears her voice saying, "Um, Daddy?"

We pulled up to the nursing home and Dad let us out on the sidewalk before he parked the car. I stood there looking at the building and remembering the last time I'd been there, when the BSC was in the midst of another mystery. We came to visit an old man who was the only living person who could tell us the truth about this house we thought might be haunted. Come to think of it, we never did learn the *whole* truth about that house.

Stoneybrook Manor is a nice-looking place — kind of homey, even though it's obviously an institution of some kind. It's all one story, with lots of big windows. There are flowers planted up and down the walkways, and places where people can sit outside and enjoy the sun. That day an old woman was taking a stroll in her walker, with a nurse by her side. She seemed to be enjoying the flowers.

We waited for Dad, and then we entered the lobby. The boys started to play in the revolving door, but I made them quit before they got too wild. Dad went to the reception desk and told the man there that we'd come to visit Joe Pike.

"Oh, yes," said the man, smiling. "He's expecting you. His room is just down the hall there, second one on the left."

We followed Dad down the hall. Suddenly I felt nervous about seeing Uncle Joe. What if he was in one of his crankier moods? I could see that some of the younger kids were beginning to feel uneasy, too. They were suddenly very, very quiet.

I walked along, trying not to look into the rooms that we passed. It must be really hard to have any privacy when you're in a nursing home. A lot of the people who were sitting around in wheelchairs weren't really even dressed — they were just in these pajama-like things. They looked at us as we walked by, and the sight of our huge family made a lot of them smile. I had a feeling that some of those people were pretty lonely. I smiled back at a couple of them, and I saw Claire waving at one old man. Was Uncle Joe feeling lonely? I started to feel better about seeing him.

We reached his room, and even though the door was open Dad knocked on it just to let Uncle Joe know we were there. He was sitting in the middle of the room, across a table from another old man. They were playing Scrabble. Uncle Joe looked up, and when he saw us he actually smiled!

"Well," he said. "Come in, come in. Don't just stand there!" Despite the smile, he could still sound cranky.

We drifted in and arranged ourselves around the room. I perched on the radiator with Claire on my lap. Uncle Joe put some tiles on the board. "Jolt," he said. "And the

'J' is on a triple letter square. That's twenty-seven points for me!" He rubbed his hands together. "I'm going to have to stop now, though," he said, "since my family is here."

His family! I felt honored that he thought of us that way.

"Let me introduce my roommate," he said to Dad. "This is Mr. Connor."

Mr. Connor nodded and smiled.

Dad jumped up and introduced all of us, probably so that Uncle Joe wouldn't have to try to remember our names. "You really don't have to stop your game, though," he said to Uncle Joe. "We can wait for you to finish, if you'd like."

Uncle Joe had already gotten up from the table. "That's all right," he said. Then he lowered his voice to a not-very quiet whisper. "He cheats, anyway," he added.

Mom and I exchanged a look. We were both trying not to laugh. Poor Mr. Connor. I'm sure he heard what Uncle Joe said! "Well," said Mom brightly, and I knew she was going to try to change the subject. "Would you like to show us around before dinner?"

We had arranged with the staff to stay for Sunday dinner. Residents of Stoneybrook Manor are allowed to invite family or friends to eat with them, as long as they reserve space ahead of time.

"Certainly," said Uncle Joe. "Now, where are my encyclopedias?"

What was he talking about? I didn't see any encyclopedias.

Fortunately, Dad noticed that Uncle Joe was patting the pockets of his suit-jacket. "Are you looking for your glasses, Uncle Joe?" he asked gently.

"Yes," replied Uncle Joe. "Didn't I just say so?" He reached into one last pocket and found them. "Here they are," he said. "Now, shall we go?"

As we followed Uncle Joe down the hall, Mom whispered to me that forgetting the names of things — or substituting other words that don't necessarily make sense — is another symptom of Alzheimer's disease. Weird.

Uncle Joe showed us around Stoneybrook Manor, and we ended up in the piano room with a few minutes to kill before dinner. There was a hubbub in one corner of the room, and I decided to see what was going on. Some young people were there, holding cats and dogs — and one *adorable* black puppy — so that the old people could pat them. "What's going on?" I asked one of the girls, who was trying to chase down a kitten.

"We're volunteers from the Humane Society," she said. "We bring animals from the pound every week. The people here love it."

Uncle Joe joined us. "I spent some time with that puppy last week," he said. "It's been a long, long time since I held a puppy on my lap!"

I thought that program sounded like a really neat idea. Maybe I could be a volunteer for it some day.

"Time for dinner," said a nurse, poking her head into the room. "Oh, hello, Mr. Pike." She smiled at us. "He's a dear," she said to me. "On his good days, anyway."

I guess we'd come on one of his *best* days. Uncle Joe seemed to be happier here at Stoneybrook Manor. The nursing home was a lot calmer than our house, and it was probably easier for him to be around other old people.

The visit went surprisingly well, I thought. But at dinner there was one last surprise. After we'd all been served our platefuls of turkey and stuffing, Uncle Joe whipped out a small red bottle and shook it all over his food. I was the only one who saw him do it, and he caught me looking. He leaned over and put his face next to mine. "Hot sauce," he whispered to me. "I had one of the nurses bring it in for me. Can't stand boring food!"

I couldn't wait to tell Mom.

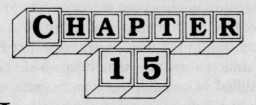

CHAPTER 15

"Hi, Mallory," said the young woman who answered the Craines' door. She smiled at me.

It took me a second to remember who she was. Then it came to me. "Aunt Bu — I mean Ellen!" I said. "Hi!" I looked down at her leg. "You got your cast off!" I exclaimed.

"Yup," she said. "What a relief! Now the doctor just wants me take it easy for about a week. After that, I'll be back on my motor-cycle."

"And you'll be ready to sit for the girls, too, I bet," I said. I followed Ellen into the kitchen, feeling kind of let down. I'd known that this was a temporary job, but I felt sad about it ending.

"I will," she said. "But I'm sure there's no way they're going to say good-bye to you just because I'm back. They've let me know they want you to sit for them once in a while."

"Oh, that's great!" I said. "I mean, if it's okay with you."

"It's fine with me. As soon as the weather gets nicer I'm going to want to be out riding a lot anyway."

I tried to imagine how it would feel to ride a motorcycle. Probably really fun, but also scary. I thought it was pretty cool that Ellen could do it. I also knew that Mom would never in a million years let *me* get a motorcycle, even if I was twenty-nine years old and living on my own!

I was just about to ask Ellen how she learned to ride a motorcycle when Margaret burst into the room. "Mallory!" she said. "Guess what!"

"Um," I said, "let's see. There's an elephant in the kitchen?"

"*Mal*lory," she said, putting her hands on her hips. Ellen stifled a giggle.

"Well, if that's not it, then I don't know," I said. "I can't guess. Tell me."

"We got a cat!" yelled Sophie, who had followed Margaret into the kitchen.

"Sophie!" cried Margaret, furious. "*I* was going to tell."

"Wow!" I said quickly. "When did you get it?"

"The other day. After that man came to pick up Ghost Ca — I mean, Rasputin. Right after you left, we got it."

"Really?" I asked.

Margaret nodded. "Daddy took me and Sophie and Katie to the animal shelter, and he said we could pick out a cat."

"Tell Mallory who saw the cat first," said Ellen.

"Katie did," said Margaret. "We were all looking at these other cats, but she walked right up to this one cage and said, 'dost tat!' So we came over to look."

"Dost tat!" echoed Katie, rubbing her eyes. She had just woken up from a nap.

"Was it really Ghost Cat?" I asked. I knew that the man had just picked Ghost Cat up, but the cat stuff had been so weird. I was ready to believe anything.

"Of course not," said Margaret. "But she does look a little like him. Come see!" She grabbed my hand and pulled me toward the laundry room. "We decided to make her a bed in here, since Ghost Cat liked it so much." She opened the door and I peeked in. A beautiful white cat was curled up on the dryer, where Ghost Cat used to sleep. She woke up when the door opened, and looked at me.

"Wow!" I said. "She's got blue eyes, just like you and your sisters. I never saw a cat with blue eyes before. She's beautiful!"

"I know," said Margaret. "That's what we

thought. Katie found the most beautiful cat in the whole animal shelter."

"Here, kittykittykitty," I said. I was dying to pick her up and feel her soft-looking fur. But the cat ignored me.

"She can't hear you," said Margaret.

"What do you mean?" I asked. "Wasn't I calling her loudly enough?"

"She couldn't hear you no matter how loudly you called," said Ellen from behind me. "She's deaf."

"A deaf cat?" I asked. "I never heard of that before."

"It's funny," said Ellen. "Lots of white cats with blue eyes are deaf. Nobody knows why."

"Wow," I said. "Does she need a lot of special care?"

"Nope!" said Margaret. "She just has to be an indoor cat, since she can't hear cars."

"The people at the shelter were really glad to find a good home for her," said Ellen. "Not everybody wants a deaf cat, even one that's as beautiful as this one."

"She *is* pretty," I said. I stroked her fur. "She's so soft!"

"Hey, girls," said Ellen. "I've got to go. How about some special good-bye hugs?" She bent down and gave each girl a big hug. "My brother will be home by five," she said to me.

Her brother? For a minute I didn't know

who she was talking about. Then I realized she meant Mr. Craine. "Oh, right!" I said. "Okay!"

Ellen left, but the girls and I stayed in the laundry room, talking about their new cat.

"Don't you want to know her name?" asked Margaret.

"Of course I do!" I said. I'd been so distracted by the news of her deafness that I'd forgotten to ask.

"Tinkerbell!" said Sophie and Margaret.

"Get it?" asked Margaret. "She's kind of named after the other cat, Tinker. But since she's a girl, she's Tinker*bell*!"

"That's a perfect name," I said.

"You know what's really funny?" asked Margaret. "Since the night that Rasputin went away and Tinkerbell came to live with us, we haven't heard that meowing noise from upstairs. Not once!"

"Hmmm . . ." I said. "That *is* kind of funny." I wondered what it meant. Was Ghost Cat really a ghost after all — the ghost of Tinker? Or was the man who came to *get* him a ghost? Or both? Did the Craines put the ghost of Tinker to rest by bringing Tinkerbell home? It was frustrating to realize I'd never know for sure. But it was also fun to have a mystery to chew on.

* * *

159

Later that afternoon, I headed over to Claud's for a BSC meeting. I couldn't wait to give everyone the latest installment in the Ghost Cat mystery. I ran up the stairs and burst into Claud's room, only to find that I'd gotten there early. The only ones there so far were Claudia herself, who naturally doesn't have any trouble getting to meetings on time; and Kristy, who is extremely punctual.

"Hi, you guys!" I said, taking my usual place on the floor.

"Hi, Mallory," said Kristy. "Come here and see what Claud's doing. You're not going to believe this."

Claudia had lined up three bottles of nail polish on her night table: one red, one white, and one black. She sat cross-legged on her bed, concentrating hard on what she was doing, but she looked up and smiled at me. "Nail designs," she said. "Everybody's doing it."

Everybody? Claudia was the first one I'd seen. But she's often the first of my friends to try new things. Anyway, you wouldn't believe Claud's nails. She wasn't just painting them — she was making designs on them! Each nail had a face on it, and each face was different. And, as usual with anything at all artistic, Claud was doing an incredible job. Her left pinky had a happy face on it. Her right thumb had an angry face. Her right ring finger looked kind of worried.

"Wow," I said. "I love that sad one. Will you do *my* nails sometime?"

"Sure," she answered. "Or if you want, I'll teach you how to do it yourself. It's not too hard."

By that time, the other members of the club had drifted in. Stacey plopped down next to Claud on the bed and picked up the bottle of red polish. "Mind if I use this?" she asked Claudia. Claud shook her head, and Stacey got to work. Jessi came in and I sat on the floor next to her. Dawn and Mary Anne arrived last and found their places just in time.

"Order!" said Kristy. Claudia's digital clock had clicked to five-thirty. The meeting had begun. We took care of club business pretty quickly: Stacey reported on how much money was in the treasury; Mary Anne asked a few questions about scheduling; and Kristy made an announcement about a new story hour that she'd heard about, which was starting that Saturday at the library. Then the phone rang.

"Hello?" asked Stacey, who'd been the first to dive for the phone. "Baby-sitters Club." She listened for a minute. "Okay, Mrs. Korman. I'm sure we can have somebody there." She hung up. "Mrs. Korman needs a sitter for Friday night," she said.

"Not me!" said Kristy. "I've had enough of Melody-the-cat for a while. Anyway, I have a job at the Perkinses'."

"Oh!" said Dawn. "That reminds me. I haven't gotten around to writing it in the club notebook yet, but when I sat at the Kormans' on Thursday, Melody wasn't a cat anymore."

"That's a relief," said Kristy.

"Well, maybe," said Dawn. "The thing is, she decided to be a fish, instead!"

We all cracked up. "How does she do *that*?" asked Kristy.

"She just walks around making swimming motions with her hands, and kissy-faces with her mouth," said Dawn, giggling. "I didn't even try to stop her, I was so grateful that she wasn't meowing!"

After we'd decided who would take the job and Stacey had called back Mrs. Korman, I told everybody about the latest on the Ghost Cat mystery. They were all fascinated, Dawn especially. She asked me about the man who had come to pick up the cat, and said she was positive he was a ghost.

"I don't know about the man," I said. "But I'm pretty sure a ghost is involved *somehow*. Anyway, it's good that the Craine girls are happy with Tinkerbell."

"You're going to miss those girls, aren't

you?" asked Mary Anne. She's always *so* sensitive to other people's feelings.

"I am," I said. "But I still have another week of sitting for them, and even after that I think I'll be seeing them now and then. You know who I do miss already, though? Uncle Joe."

Jessi reached out and touched my shoulder. "Just think, though," she said. "At least he's being taken care of, and he's comfortable. There are even things he *likes* about being at Stoneybrook Manor."

"You're right," I replied. "At least he's not spending the rest of his days like old Kennedy Graham, all alone in a big old house and going crazy because his cat has died."

The meeting went on, but I kind of tuned out for the rest of it. I was thinking about Uncle Joe, and planning my next visit to Stoneybrook Manor. Maybe the Craine girls would like to come with me sometime. We could even bring Tinkerbell. . . .

About the Author

ANN M. MARTIN did *a lot* of baby-sitting when she was growing up in Princeton, New Jersey. She is a former editor of books for children, and was graduated from Smith College.

Ms. Martin lives in New York City with her cats, Mouse and Rosie. She likes ice cream and *I Love Lucy*; and she hates to cook.

Ann Martin's Apple Paperbacks include *Yours Turly, Shirley*; *Ten Kids, No Pets*; *With You and Without You*; *Bummer Summer*; and all the other books in the Baby-sitters Club series.

THE BABY-SITTERS CLUB

Look for Mystery #4

KRISTY AND THE MISSING CHILD

Suddenly I just felt incredibly sad about the whole thing. "You know, whatever happened to Jake, this whole experience must be really hard on him." I thought of Jake, and how scared or confused — or both — he must be. And before I knew it, my eyes filled up with tears and one of them had spilled over. I could have died! I *never* cry in front of anyone. That's Mary Anne's thing, crying. But I'm different. I'm Kristy. I'm tough.

"Kristy," Bart said. "It's going to be okay." He leaned toward me. I closed my eyes.

"Hey, you guys!" yelled Karen as she slammed the door open and ran into the den. "Jake's on TV!"

My eyes popped open. "Jake?" I asked. "Jake's on TV? You mean they found him?" I sat up straight.

"No," said Karen. "Just his *picture* is on TV. They're talking about how he's missing." She leaned down and turned on the little TV that we keep in the den. "See?"

Jake's face filled the screen. I felt my stomach tighten up when I saw his big brown eyes. I recognized the picture that was being shown: It was Jake's school picture, which I'd last seen hanging on the wall in the Kuhns' front hall. The TV people had superimposed the word MISSING, in red, over his chest.

**Don't miss any of the latest books
in The Baby-sitters Club series
by Ann M. Martin**

168

THE BABY-SITTERS CLUB®

by Ann M. Martin

The Baby-sitters' business is booming! And that gets Stacey, Kristy, Claudia, and the rest of The Baby-sitters Club members in all kinds of adventures...at school, with boys, and, of course, baby-sitting!

Something new and exciting happens in every Baby-sitters Club book. Collect and read them all!

More titles... ▶

The Baby-sitters Club titles continued...

Available wherever you buy books...or use this order form.

Scholastic Inc., P.O. Box 7502, 2931 E. McCarty Street, Jefferson City, MO 65102

Please send me the books I have checked above. I am enclosing $_____
(please add $2.00 to cover shipping and handling). Send check or money order - no cash or C.O.D.s please.

Name _____

Address _____

City _____ State/Zip _____